DARLING SAVAGE SINS

ALSO BY DV FISCHER

Forbid Me Not

Bouquet of Lies

Bed of Roses

Field of Lilies

DARLING SAVAGE SINS

USA TODAY BESTSELLING AUTHOR

DV FISCHER

LNP

Darling Savage Sins
Paperback Edition

Love N. Books Press
An Imprint of Wolfpack Publishing
1707 E. Diana Street
Tampa, FL 33610

www.lovenbookspress.com

Edited by My Brother's Editor

Paperback ISBN 979-8-89567-647-9
Ebook ISBN 979-8-89567-646-2

PLAYLIST

1. Leftovers by Dennis Lloyd
2. Done All Wrong by Black Rebel Motorcycle Club
3. Bad Habits by (Rock Cover by No Resolve)
4. Blood // Water by Grandson
5. Make it Lower by Carpetman
6. Devil Eyes by Hippie Sabotage

DARLING SAVAGE SINS

CHAPTER ONE
JAGGER VALENTINE

THIS BAR'S stools are fucking heavy.

Its thick legs scrape against the bar's worn-out wood floor as I push it back with the back of my thighs, and I stand up fully. The music and the high volume of people's chatter beat against my chest in an unwelcome way.

I have to get out of here. I can't fucking breathe.

I keep my eye on my empty glass for a moment while I pull out my pack of cigarettes from my jeans pocket. Bending at the hip and leaning to my right, I shout in Blake's ear. His curly red hair tickles my nose as I say, "I'll be right back." I don't wait for his reply before I swivel and weave between the crowd, passing by a speaker that's playing a catchy rock song. That song came out before I was born,

By the back exit, there's a couple deep in a private conversation, and they gracefully move out of my way. I push through the heavy door until the warm summer air embraces the bare skin of my arms and of my face. The door whooshes closed behind me, cutting off the majority of the bar's battering sounds.

Silence. Thank fuck.

Tipping my head back, I stare at the stars and soak in their normalcy and comfort.

As someone in the Army, I've seen the stars from every corner of the earth and have traveled more places than I can count. But here, in the semi-small town of Ashland, Oregon, it hits a little different. These are home's stars. They know the brutal secrets of my past, and they know the sinful secrets I carried home from across the pond this last deployment.

I bring the pack of smokes up to my chest, flip the top, and pick out the lucky cigarette for this evening. I don't smoke often, but tonight felt right. The harder stuff would be better, but I'm never the one who finds a dealer or who even knows who and where they are. That's Blake's department, and he holds me on such a tight leash that he only provides such things if I'm having a particularly nasty night.

I light the cigarette, take a puff, and exhale while mouthing "PTSD."

That's what they call it. That's what they told me when I came home a month ago and pulled a gun on the first person who spooked me. Turned out it was my neighbor who had come to check on me because my mail had piled up outside my apartment door. It was a shit show. I had to beg the landlord to get to stay in that apartment. I didn't, however, plead with the police to not take me away for a few weeks and lock me behind bars for pulling the weapon in the first place. But I had gotten off easy, and I suspect it has everything to do with the judge's daughter having been in my unit.

Small mercies. I don't get those often, so I kept my mouth shut and did my time in county jail, considering it a vacation.

Ever since then, Blake checks on me several times a day. He was also in my unit, but somehow he didn't come home all fucked up. He has his head on straight. Either that, or he hides it a hell of a lot better than I can.

He didn't have to do everything I did, however. I was the monster at the end of the government's leash. He was the one who came in and cleaned up what I'd done in the name of my country.

The back door opens as I deeply inhale my cigarette, and Blake slides out of the opening he created. He leans against the brick wall of the bar, observing me and my state of mind. I hold the smoke in and let the burn soothe the fire within me.

"What is it this time?" Blake asks quietly.

I glance at him and blow the smoke toward the sky. "Too many sounds."

He stuffs his hands in his pockets and lowers his eyes toward the tips of his shoes. Blake is almost as tall as me and just as heavily packed with muscle. That's where our similarities end. His curled hair is closely cut to his head like a typical army gentleman, but as soon as I got home, I let mine grow. The dirty-blond top is several inches long, styled to the southeast of my head, with the sides of my head shaved. It was the first thing I could think of to rebel against what I'd done.

"You have to get used to sounds at some point, man."

I point my cigarette in his direction. "It's a lot better than it used to be."

He contemplates me from a sideways look. "What about—"

I swipe my hand through the air, anger immediately taking hold and gripping something tightly in my chest. I should have known this is where the conversation would lead. "I will not be going to therapy," I growl.

We both look as a figure moves through the dark down the back street, homeless if I had to guess.

Blake quiets his voice. "You've been home for a month, and you haven't settled down. You know it'd help."

"I don't give a shit what you think."

"You're drinking every night, you can't sleep, everything reminds you of what…what they asked you to do."

I note that he didn't say "us." I almost correct him, but he carries on.

"You're lost, dude. It's a miracle you haven't ate a bullet yet."

I stare at the cherry of my cigarette, slowly spinning my wrist this way and that to study it fully while the trickle of rising smoke tickles the bridge of my nose. "I have no interest in death."

Blake mumbles something about my habits being a slow death under his breath, but then more loudly says, "I'll get you some water."

"I'm fine."

"You're wasted. I've been watching you sway since I got out here."

"I am not swaying."

I don't have to look at him to know he's rolling his eyes. "I'm getting you some water."

I don't reply as he heads inside. Instead, I continue to study the dwindling cigarette. In the back of my mind, I can hear the homeless man walk closer, but I pay him no mind. Something he's carrying rattles, but again, I shove it out of my mind. I continue to stare at the cherry, marveling at how it looks like the embers of what's left of the house fires we created to flush out who we needed. I get so engrossed in it that when the homeless man's bag crashes to the ground before me, I shut down. The sound…oh god the sound…

The only thing I'm aware of is my ears screaming from my rapid blood flow.

Time stands still for a minute, and in those seconds, I don't feel, I don't see, I don't sense. I can count the heartbeats if I wanted to, locked in this pocket of my mind that I am. A place that's equally terrifying and peaceful.

"Jag!"

It comes through the fog, pushing past the rhythmic thrum in my ears.

"Jag!"

Louder this time. Something touches my arm. Nails scrape against my skin.

"Goddammit, Jag. Let him go!"

And then my vision returns.

I have the back of the homeless man to my chest, my arms wrapped around his neck. His arms hang loosely at his sides, and his neck no longer holds up his greasy head.

Blake is pulling at my arms, fear etched around the set of his eyes.

Startled, I let go of the man, and he crumbles next to the bag he had dropped. For a moment, we both stare at the body, our breathing the only sound this late at night. I should feel something. Anything. All I feel is…nothing.

Blake starts cursing under his breath. Using both hands, he shoves me in the shoulder. "This isn't the enemy territory, Jag!"

I swipe a hand down my face to hide that my fingers are shaking from the copious amounts of adrenaline coursing under my skin.

"You can't just go around killing people, dammit!" he continues in a hiss, shoving me again. He begins pacing, tugging at what little curls are available on his head. "You are so fucked up. Beyond fucked up." He turns to me and opens his arms wide, encompassing the world. "How can I help you, Jag? Tell me, because I'm out of fucking ideas."

"We have to get the body off the road," I murmur, still staring at what I'd done. I should feel something, anything, but I don't. All I feel are the lasting effects of my blackout, the adrenaline mostly. I wait for that feeling to come, that remorse. Maybe even guilt or shame. I'd have to wait for eternity. Perhaps eternity will be what it takes, when I stand before God and he questions me on the man that I am.

"Jesus fucking Christ," he whispers. Perhaps he's just now realizing that no one can help me. He should have known that the moment our plane landed back in the country. "And what exactly are we going to do with the body, Jag? Hmm? This is home! We don't leave them out in the open! Hell, we shouldn't even have to leave them anywhere because it shouldn't happen!"

I glance around, utter calmness embracing me like an old lover as I begin to calculate what I think is a level-headed plan. Is this who I am now? A monster? I knew I was a monster, but I've been starting to think I wasn't made one but born one. From the people I came from, surely that hypothesis is correct, because the Middle East didn't make me, it developed—preyed—on what was already there in the first place.

Blake doesn't get it. He never will.

"Go get the car."

"And then what?" he growls.

Finally, I turn to him, expression blank because I still don't feel a damn thing. "Put him in the trunk. Ashland is surrounded by National Forest, asshole. We'll dump him off the beaten path, and by the time someone finds him, he'll be nothing but bones thanks to the wildlife."

He stares at me for a moment, taking me in, truly considering the man before him. "I can't believe I'm doing this," he murmurs in awe before heading to the body and bending to grab the man's feet. "Grab his fucking arms, Jag."

CHAPTER TWO
DOLLY STERLING

FOUR MONTHS LATER

A RARE FALL storm rages outside, pounding against the gym's many large windows. The gym is dim, but every lightning strike brightens it up for a split second. It creates such an eerie feeling.

Sweat drips down my neck like the rain on the panes as I swing my fist again and again at the punching bag dangling before me.

"Right, right, left," Rollo says from behind the bag. He's keeping it from swaying, waiting on the other side for me to pummel the bag the best my chubby fists can.

Strands of my long unbound brown hair stick to the sides of my face with every single swing, and with much annoyance, I have to keep swiping it away. I do exactly as he says, taking in all his instruction. He's taken self-defense most of his life, and now that he's been a cop for the past decade, he makes sure his skills remain sharp by giving a few people lessons a couple times a week. I, his ex-wife, happen to be one of them. My—our—best friend happens to be another.

"Good!" he says, and then he straightens. "Let's take a break."

I don't think I will ever need to defend myself,

however much Rollo tries to say otherwise. I may be a therapist, but that doesn't make all my clients crazy bastards. Most are just people trying to survive. He won't hear that, though. He's a good guy and just wants me safe. I get that, and truth be told, the exercise is good for me anyway.

He steps away from the bag, and I get a view of his profile. There's barely any sweat on his oval face, but a fine sheen is across his toned arms. His dark head of hair is disheveled like it always is at the gym. When he's on the job, it's combed neatly to the side like a proper gentleman. His features are more baby-faced than they are rugged, however, and I've always teased him about that fact, until he grew that beard. The facial hair was a game changer for him.

I put my hands above my head, resting my wrists on the top of my crown. "So soon?"

He chuckles and shakes his head, and we both head to the bench where our water bottles and sweat towels are resting. "Oh, shut up. Don't pretend like you don't need one. You sound like a dying cow."

I grab my water bottle from his waiting hand and glare at him. But I cannot deny that I do sound like a dying animal by the way that I'm wheezing. "I'm still out of shape."

A smirk takes over his face. "I'm sorry that the divorce was so hard on you that you let yourself go, Dolly."

I give him a playful shove. We both know that the divorce started and ended on friendly terms. We both agreed that we had fallen out of love and would rather be great friends than pretend lovers. Neither of us has remarried. He hasn't even started dating yet, but that's not because he doesn't want to. The right one just hasn't come along, I guess. And as for me? I've dated. They just end up leaving me behind as soon as they get what they want.

Our meeting wasn't much of a fairy tale. We had met at a college party, and we kept bumping into each other after that. It wasn't long until he asked me on our first date. I was much skinnier then, though.

I gesture to my body, which is ample with a few extra layers of flesh and punctuated with thick rounded curves. "We both know I didn't give a rat's ass about my weight when we were married."

"Neither did I." He picks up his water bottle and takes a swig. "But you did care in college when you started putting it on."

Talking about this with anyone else would likely hurt my feelings, but since I've seen Rollo naked, it just feels like normal conversation.

"Yeah, well, that was fifteen years ago. A lot changes when you get married. People let shit go, and for me, one of them happened to be my body." The other was my sanity for how many times he missed the toilet or how many times he got toothpaste all over the counter. Let's also not forget the nose hair trimmings he'd leave peppered all around the faucet, but I'm not going to bring that up today. I'll keep those in my arsenal for a later date.

"I see you trying." For a moment, he contemplates me over the curve of his bottle, mid-swig. "So why now?"

I give him a little shrug and swipe my towel from the bench. As I dab my forehead, I admit, "I don't have a protector around, and if I'm going to be able to defend myself, like you keep nagging about, I need to actually maybe somewhat try to lose some weight. Right?"

"You're not doing it to just satisfy me?"

I shake my head and then give a little shrug. "I don't care about the defending much, and frankly, I'm not *that* big. I just want to be able to take care of myself and not have a heart attack when I'm running from a soon-to-be rapist."

He rolls his eyes at my dramatics. Ashland is small, and the sexual assault crimes are even smaller. "So then get yourself another guy."

I laugh out loud, but it's more of a nervous laugh than anything else. I could say that I don't need a guy, that I can take care of myself, but we both know that I don't like being alone. That and dick is a food group for me. "The only people I have conversations with are you, Sadie, and my clients. I don't see you and I trying to date again, Sadie has the wrong sex organs, and my clients are…well, it's unethical, and most of them are disturbed."

"That's what you get for being a therapist," he says, poking my shoulder.

"A life of solitude?"

"Yeah. All you have time for is your clients, and by the time you're done helping them, you have no interest in meeting someone new."

"I met Sadie," I say, tossing my wet towel at him.

He cringes as it slaps him in the cheek. "A homeless girl you helped get off the streets doesn't count. You still haven't told me that full story, and we were married at the time. Neither has she, for that matter."

I set my water bottle down and start stretching my arms. I can already tell that we're done working out for the day and that he'd rather chat instead. I don't mind. If I continue on with the workout, I'll be too sore to move tomorrow anyway. "It's her story to tell. Besides, she's my best friend."

"She wasn't at the time. She was a stranger. And she's my best friend too, dickwad."

"Yeah, well…" I stop the conversation there, just like I

always do. Sadie Watt's life story is her own, and it never felt right to share it with anyone else. Such a dark past she holds. Such trauma and fear. It wouldn't be fair to her if I go around sharing the horror story that was her life, even if Rollo is also her best friend. She can tell him if she wants, but I'm not going to.

Knowing that that's all I'll give him, which is nothing, he sits on the bench and slides off his shoes. "Are you and Sadie going out tonight then?"

I place my hands on my hips. "As a matter of fact, we are."

He chuckles under his breath. "Predictable. You know, that'll be what gets you in the end; your routine is the same. It's so the same that I don't even have to live in the same house as you, and I know it by heart. If you get attacked, it'll be for that reason."

"What?"

He points at me. "You go to the same bar. You shop at the same store. You find peace in the same areas. Catch my drift?"

"Maybe you should come get drinks with us then, if you're so worried about the safety of my boring life."

He wrinkles his nose at me. "No thanks."

I was expecting that answer. Bars were never his scene, even the laid-back ones.

I playfully slap the back of my hand on his chest. "I'm not the only one who is predictable."

"Mm-hmm," he hums. He bends and grabs his gym bag from under the bench, slips his shoes inside, and pulls out sandals.

"Your feet are going to get soaked, bud." I point to the window where the rain pelts the building.

"I don't want to ruin my shoes."

I grab my sweat towel from the floor where it had

fallen and toss it in the nearby laundry basket. "You and your damn shoes."

I take a seat on the bench beside him and bump my shoulder against his. He bumps me back.

After a few moments of listening to the storm, he quietly asks, "You know, I wasn't making a dig at you for being a therapist, right?"

I frown at the side of his face. "Oh god, Rollo. Of course, I know."

"Good." He tugs on a brown strand of my hair. "Because honestly, Dolly, I had no reason to be, but I was a messed-up teen before I met you. I had a normal life with a normal family, and I was still messed up. My brain was a fucking mess, and as you learned how to heal people, you healed me too."

My frown only deepens. "Why are you telling me this?"

"So you know how good you are at it, and...so you understand that I think I had clung to you because you were so healing. I think I mistook that as love. And once you healed me, I realized that. I don't want you thinking you couldn't save us or any of that kind of bullshit some exes go through."

I laugh out loud and then quickly become somber when I realize he's being serious. Sighing, I push the hair from my sticky cheeks. "I've had time to think about this. I have come to the conclusion that I have a thing for the savage and damaged minds. I knew your mind was a problem when we started dating—I was attracted to it. You're not the first damaged boy I've run across, and you haven't been the last. And once you healed, well...you became boring."

He glares at me. "I am not boring."

I point at my chest. "I'm predictable, and you, sir, are boring."

He shakes his head, but he can't hide his grin. When the grin fades, he gives me a serious and stern look, and I know then and there that he's going to give me a tiny lecture. "I don't mind that you're not dating boring men right now, and I'm glad that you realize your weakness when it comes to men, but I worry that if you wait too long to get back on that dating horse and look for the right guy, you'll make a huge mistake and fall for the first guy who flirts your way. We've been down that road, and none have ended well. And who knows what kind of fucked up he'll be this time around?"

I point at him. "You're not dating either, big guy."

He slaps my finger away, but I don't miss the sheepish look on his face. "I've at least thought about it. Have you?"

I give a little shrug. "Not really. But when the opportunity comes along, let's both pray that he's a normal, mentally healthy guy."

He chuffs. "Damn right. The last thing I need is to make sure these lessons aren't for the real possibility that you'll use them."

"I'm not stupid enough to get involved with someone violent. I work with those types of people every day. I know them by glance."

He reaches and squeezes the point of my knee. "Good. Good. Seriously though, try dating again. We both should. It'll be healthy and shit."

"Do you have someone in mind?"

"Maybe. Do you?"

"Nope." I grab my water bottle and my jacket from under the bench and stand. "I'll think about it." And then I lean down and peck him on the cheek. "I have to go. Sadie is probably already waiting for me."

He ignores the saliva I left on his cheek, even as I start backing away toward the door and sliding my jacket on.

"On second thought," he calls after me. "Let me attend the first date so that I can make sure you're not dating a fuckwad."

"Bye, Rollo," I say mid-laugh.

"I'm serious, Dolly!" he shouts after me, but I'm already pushing through the door and headed out toward the rain.

CHAPTER THREE
JAGGER VALENTINE

THERE'S ONLY one reason I didn't bring Blake to this bar, and that reason is that I'm tired of the looks he's been giving me for the past few months. The disapproval. Perhaps even disgust.

He doesn't fucking get it. No one does.

Right now, he doesn't even know I'm out of my apartment. He thinks I took some sleeping pills the doctor prescribed me two months ago and that I'm at my apartment, safe in bed and sound asleep. Little does he know, I'm here every night. Every bartender who works here knows what I order by now, and every time they fulfill that order, Blake's voice rattles in the back of my head, the one that tells me I have a problem.

I know he's not wrong.

But I also don't give a shit.

How I choose to numb the pain isn't a bad thing in my book. How is my pain from my childhood colliding with my pain from the military not supposed to affect me?

What do I have to live for anymore besides the one person that I left behind? What is there left for me but nightmares in the day and screaming in the night? Aside from my trauma, I'm eaten by guilt. The chances of getting the person I care about away from where she's trapped are a long shot, even though it's why I came back to this wretched town in the first place.

In the dark corner of the bar and on the chipped wood surface of the high table I sit at, I stare at my hands, twisting my wrists until the lines of my palms play with the shadows. There's been a lot of blood on these hands, blood I've had to dig out of my nails. Flashes of the eyes I've stared into before taking their life flit through my mind, because that is all I remember: their eyes. The shades. The swirls. The fear. It's punctuated by the sounds of the whip from my childhood.

I don't remember my victims' faces, and certainly not their names. But I do remember the welts from the whip with utter clarity.

My hands begin shaking, and to stop the flashing, colliding memories, I quickly grab my whiskey and gulp a generous sip. The burn travels down my throat, and it takes everything I have to lift my eyes to the inside of the bar and still not see the blood, the blown-wide pupils.

There aren't many people here tonight, but it isn't often that this bar is busy. Fridays are usually more packed than any other day, so I avoid that night of the week, choosing to drink outside of my apartment building on the front step instead.

There's a man sitting on one side of the bar who is watching a sports game, and an older, more rugged man on the other side staring at the female bartender. In front of the window that the rain is beating against is a gaggle of annoying young women dressed too finely for a place like this. They've looked my way a few times, giggled as one in particular made fuck-me eyes in my direction. I know I'm attractive, I'm often told so, but I won't be taking her up on that offer. She's too young and too inexperienced to handle someone like me, to handle my needs. Don't get me wrong, I want someone tonight—the thought presses against every corner of my brain—but I like my women bigger, and I won't settle for anything less. I need something to grab onto, some bounce as I plow into them.

With all those people accounted for, I swivel my gaze to the last remaining table. Two women about my age—in their early thirties—sit at this table, leaning close to each other and laughing hysterically under their breath at some joke the other made. There's a skinny blonde covered in tattoos whose face I cannot see and a thicker brunette who faces me. I don't know why, but I fixate on the brunette. She has a defined jaw, the most perfect peach-colored full lips I've ever seen, and from where I sit, her eyes are dark blue. Bangs cover her eyebrows, and her long hair is twisted in a ringlet that rests along her right breast. As far as I can tell, she doesn't wear makeup, and that piques my interest because there's nothing sexier than a woman with the confidence to not need makeup.

The way she smiles is hypnotizing. Such pure and undiluted joy on her face and in the way she holds herself. I can tell she's generally the quiet type, and I know from experience that it's the quiet type that surprises you.

With my interest fully piqued, I watch her discreetly for a while until eventually she catches on and starts glancing in my direction. At first, I hold her gaze for a split second and then look away. We play this game for a bit until I finally hold it for heartbeats longer and give her a punctuating smirk at the end. A blush creeps over her cheeks, and she looks anywhere but at me.

I may be well on my way past drunk, but I still know *that* look. *She's interested.*

Her friend peers over her shoulder for a moment to see what has caught her friend's attention. For a split second, I think I recognize her friend, but she's turned back around before I can be sure. Besides, it wouldn't be uncommon to recognize someone in Ashland. It's not that big of a city.

The waitress comes over and gives me another drink without even asking, and I stop her before she leaves. "Do me a favor. See that brown-haired girl over there?" She looks over her shoulder. I wait for her to respond, but she doesn't, so I press on. "Can you whisper in that girl's ear and tell her I'm staring because she's stunning?"

The waitress contemplates it for a moment, then turns and does what I ask. She approaches the women, and instead of whispering it to the brunette, she speaks directly to her. Whatever. However she wants to do it is fine.

The brunette's gaze snaps to mine, and she hides her face in her hands, but I can clearly see the blush spreading out around her fingers.

The waitress comes back to my table with her hands on her hips. "The blond one told me to tell you that the other girl thinks you're hot and that you should come sit with her."

"Oh?"

I'm chuckling under my breath when the friend gets up, grabs her purse from the back of her chair, and pecks her friend on the cheek. The friend gives me a stern look that I can barely see because of the dimness of the bar, but she leaves just as quickly as the look had come.

The waitress walks away, and I get up from my chair as soon as the door whooshes closed behind the blond. I head to the brunette, and the sound of my footsteps makes her have the courage to lower her hands. Her eyes track my every movement, that blush still slightly on her cheeks.

I take a seat across from her and set my drink down in

front of me. I settle in, relaxing my posture to let her know I feel at ease. I don't greet her, I don't have some sexy saying. We simply stare at one another, daring the other to speak first. It's a fun little game, and honestly, I'd love to know how long it'd last, but I want to see what she does when I break first.

"What's your name?" My voice is quiet and rumbly, but then again, it's always rumbly.

She blinks in surprise. I get that often. My voice is deeper than most men's.

"Jesus, your voice is…um, never mind," she whispers.

I chuckle and raise an eyebrow at her because that wasn't the answer to the question I asked. "Name?"

Her gaze drifts to my lips as she says, "Dolly."

I lean into the table a little bit. "Pretty name, Dolly darling." The name is fitting. She does have that porcelain doll-type face. It's hot as fuck, making her look like my plaything for the evening.

I watch as her throat swallows. I know the "darling" nickname will stick, and I also know that it purred in my throat. The goose bumps along her arms tell me she liked it more than I thought she would.

"What's your name?" she asks, bravely returning her gaze to mine.

"Jagger, but my friends don't call me that."

"What do they call you?"

Asshole. Dick. Bastard. "Jag."

She licks her bottom lip. It's a completely unconscious thing, and she doesn't know it's sexy as hell. "I wouldn't do that," I add.

"Do what?" she asks with her brows pinching together.

"Wet your lips like that. You have no idea what it does to me. What ideas it gives me."

Crimson blotches her cheeks, and she looks away

with a smile tipping the edges of her lips. "And if I want those ideas to eventually happen?" She looks back at me, and there's a confidence there that I wasn't expecting.

"Eventually?"

"I'm going to assume I know what you want—"

"What you also want."

"But I don't just sleep with anyone."

"Then what's your rule for sleeping with someone?"

She shrugs and tucks her bottom lip between her teeth. I can't help it when I reach and pull that lip out with my thumb, then run the pad across the soft flesh.

She shivers, and I return my hand to my whiskey glass as she clears her throat and says, "Well, I have to know someone first."

"How about we both share one thing about ourselves?"

"Just one?" I can tell that disappoints her, but I'm not entirely looking for what she is, even though she's hot as hell and exactly the shape I like.

I lean a little into the table. "One thing for one night, darling."

CHAPTER FOUR
DOLLY STERLING

SLOWLY, a smile spreads across my lips. "You're trouble." He definitely is, there's no way around it. Hell, even his haircut screams bad boy, not to mention the tattoos peeking out around his clothes. I'm surprised Sadie left me with him.

He runs the back of my knuckles along his lips, and I know it's to keep me from knowing just how right I am. "You go first," he murmurs.

God, that voice. It's deep and smooth and tingles all the right places along my body.

What could I possibly tell him about myself? Should I even want to? I could do the right thing, refuse to give out any information about me, and leave, but those eyes of his are hypnotizing. They have me under their spell, and truth be told…I'd like to take him up on his offer.

I scrape my teeth over my bottom lip as Rollo's voice rings in the back of my mind, reminding me that I at least should try to meet a guy. This man before me isn't what he had in mind. However, he said nothing about one-night stands. I can tell that that's all this will be anyway, and in the end, Rollo doesn't have to know.

"Okay," I say, building some confidence under the pressure of his pheromones and the weight of his presence. I slide my drink toward my middle just so that I have something to hold on to, and then I lean a little toward him and quietly say, "I'm attracted to the wrong kind of guy."

"And what kind of guy is that?" he asks, completely intrigued. His eyes twinkle with untold mischief.

I shrug a little, as if it means nothing, but in reality, it's the solid ground on which stands my every flaw. "The savaged. The damaged."

A sly smile spreads across his face. "And what if I told you I was those things?"

I know he's telling the truth. Nice guys don't cover themselves in tattoos and hide themselves in dark corners of a bar. "Tell me something about yourself, and let me decide."

His eyes roam my face and then trace the curve of my neck. He lingers on a spot that I like bit most, as if he already knows what teeth scraping against that area feels like to me. "I have a knack for knowing what a woman wants in the bedroom."

"Oh yeah?" I ask, challenging him.

His attention moves to my lips, and his expression grows serious when he lifts his gaze to mine. "I'd know exactly where to bite you, darling," he purrs so deep that it sounds otherworldly. "When to make you bleed, when to lick the pain away. Where to suck and where to hum."

I swallow thickly, and I don't know where it comes from, because all my instincts should scream for me to run, but I bravely whisper, "Prove it." It's a demand, a call to action, a two-word plea that I'm done talking.

"Hmm," he murmurs, as if I just gave him butterflies. "Perhaps you'll be addicting."

He doesn't give me time to respond, not that I'd know what to say, before he gets up and holds out his hand for me to take. Without thinking too hard on why I'm about to do a very stupid thing, I slide my fingers into his palm, and he helps me hop down from my stool. The skin on his palm is calloused, but his grip is firm and confident as he leads me toward the door.

We're out of the bar moments later.

In the light splattering of rain, we weave between the few cars in the parking lot before he reaches a large black truck with heavily tinted windows. It's off to the right, away from all the others, just as he had been inside before he came to my table. I notice that it's conveniently out of the parking lot lights' reach, tucked in the shadows of great trees.

I can't help the giggle that bubbles up in my chest, and I relish in the smirk he gives me over his shoulder because of it.

He takes me to the passenger side. It's the side that's not facing the public, and I'm grateful for that, because as soon as we're shielded, Jagger pins me against the extended cab's door by the upper arms, bends his head, and captures my mouth. Immediately, I taste the whiskey, but there are notes of clover and honey that complement the bitter flavor of alcohol.

The way he kisses…it makes my toes curl in my shoes. He devours, conquers, and owns, and I let him because it feels so damn good to let someone else take control for a moment. His breath fans my cheeks and tickles my eyelashes, and as soon as he slides his hands down to my wrists, lifts them over my head, and pins them at the top of the truck, goose bumps rise over my skin.

He pulls away an inch, leaving me breathless, and says, "Keep your arms there."

I completely obey, and he takes the opportunity to grab the hem of my shirt and lift it over my head in one smooth motion. His mouth finds my neck as he reaches for the band of my yoga pants and thong, and slowly, oh-so-slowly, he hooks them with his thumbs and pushes them over my ass, down my thighs, letting them pool around my ankles on the wet pavement. My bra comes off next and joins my clothes on the ground.

I don't even care that putting them back on while they're wet is going to be a bitch. I just want this man to touch my bare skin.

Hungrily, he drinks me in, and the way he does it makes me feel powerful and sexy, both things that I've been missing in my life. He quickly scans my ankles and my bare legs, and then his expression shifts to hunger when he reaches my pussy. It stays there for a moment until finally, his eyes move up my stomach, flare when they reach my breasts, and are scorching once they land on my parted lips.

God, what that look does to me. That raw hunger. That pure arousal plastered on his face. I could slay the world with the way he eats me with his eyes. I've never felt so sexy before.

Finally, when he's reached some sort of conclusion, he considers me with his head slightly cocked.

I have the urge to lower my hands, but instead, I ask breathily, "What?"

He nonchalantly shrugs. "Just wondering if you can truly handle this."

"What do you mean? What do you have in mind?" There's a little bit of leeriness in my tone.

He excitedly wets his kiss-swollen lips. "I don't just want to fuck you out in the open. I want to make you bleed a little."

I scowl. Bleed? "Why?"

"I want to leave a little reminder of the mysterious stranger who hunted you down tonight."

He reaches inside his pocket, and I watch as he pulls out a pocketknife. He flicks his wrist, and the knife opens on a click. Nervousness flutters in my stomach. I'm open to different things when it comes to sex, but a knife? Carving something into someone's skin as a memento?

My eyes flare, and I stare a little too long at the blade, wondering if I should run or if I should wait to see what happens next.

"Can you handle this?" he murmurs so deep that I almost didn't catch the words.

I flick my eyes back to his and clear my throat. He's expecting an answer from me, and if I wait too long, he'll likely make the choice for me. "I've never—" I clear my throat again, trying to keep the fear out of my tone. And then it hits me. I know what this is. He's a predator in the night, a man who wants to own, devour, and discard. The therapist in me would love to know more, would soak up how he came to be so disconnected with humanity, but the woman in me—the one who is attracted to red flags—wants to know what happens next.

The latter wins.

For the first time since he put them there, I lower my hands from above my head and gently take the knife from him. I watch as his head tilts slightly to the side again, curious about what I plan to do next. I bring the tip of the knife just under my collarbone, prepared to give him exactly what he wants. His lips part as I apply pressure and gently slice. I don't have to look down to know I've cut the skin. I can feel a thin trail of blood travel down to my breast and know that's exactly what I'd done. I just hope I didn't cut too deep.

He chuckles darkly and shakes his head. "Braver than I thought you were." And I get the feeling he means more than just me cutting myself. What he's surprised at is that I remain standing before him.

"You're not going to scare me off," I murmur.

He hums at the back of his throat, and then he lowers

himself to his knees and runs his tongue around my nipple, careful to avoid the little river of blood. I shiver, and it has nothing to do with how the cold rain is sprinkling against my flushed skin. Instead, it has everything to do with the man kneeling before me, the stranger who clearly isn't finished with me yet.

He covers my nipple with his mouth and curves his tongue around it before he gives a rough suck. My head falls back, my face tilting toward the sky. The heat from his mouth makes my clit tingle, and the way he sucks my nipple makes me grab for his shoulders and curl my nails into his sweatshirt.

As if my grappling for his sweatshirt made him remember he was still wearing one, he stops sucking my breast for a moment so he can lift it and his shirt over his head and toss it to the ground with my clothes. I only get seconds to look at his body before he's on me again.

He's absolutely covered in tattoos and sprinkled in scars, so much so that question after question flits through my mind. I shove them aside, knowing that I won't get those answers, and instead, continue my quick search. His abs stick out the most, and then the bulging biceps and firm pecs. He's not overly muscular, but I can tell his body is a machine.

With my nipples thoroughly teased, he raises himself to his feet and captures my mouth again. His fingers slide down my lower abdomen, over my thick middle, and slip into the folds of my pussy. I suck in a sharp breath through my nose. I hadn't expected that sudden jolt to my clit by his single touch, and the surprise is evident. It causes him to chuckle from deep within his chest, so much so that it sounds more like a lion's purr than anything else.

Slowly, he circles my clit with two skilled fingers. It's been so long since someone touched me there that I instantly quiver. The knife drops from my hand, landing with a clunk on the pavement.

"I wonder what would happen if I carved something pretty onto your skin," he mumbles against my lips. "Something that you'll always remember me fucking you by."

I whimper as he continues to rub my most sensitive bundle of nerves, building me to the edge so damn swiftly. He hums at the back of his throat, a praise to my sounds of pleasure. His fingers circle faster as he watches me grow nearer to the peak of my climax. He's applying just the right amount of pressure, whispering all the right things in my ear, and keeping such an even pace that my thighs begin to shake and fire circles in my lower abdomen. It waits to explode with such a force that I'm not sure my legs would continue to hold me once it does.

Hell, they're barely holding me up now.

"If I picked up the knife again, would you run?" He leans until his lips brush my ear. "Would you let me chase you down and do whatever the hell I wanted to you?"

My mind goes wild with imagination. I could dart into those trees, and he could catch me and press me against the rough bark of trunks before fucking me against them.

The imagery is all it takes, and I fall apart on his fingers. I come with a scream that he captures with his mouth, angling my head with his free hand so that he can shove his tongue in my mouth to tangle with my own.

My entire body shakes as wave after wave of heat courses through my veins with absolutely nowhere to go. My toes curl painfully, and my nails dig deep into his hips, just to hold onto some resemblance of reality.

When I finally come down from my all-time high, he moves his fingers to the button of his jeans, and I break the kiss to look down, to watch as he unzips, pushes them down, and reveals the length of his cock in one smooth motion.

I gulp at the length of it and the Jacob's ladder piercing that taunts me in all the delicious ways.

"Grab it," he demands after a moment, and I do, reaching and gripping the base of him, feeling the piercings press into my palm.

I can tell he tries to hold back the moan, but it comes from deep within him anyway.

His hand slides down my ass to the back of my thigh, and he lifts my knee and hooks it around his hip. By now, the rain is pelting us, but I'm determined to keep my leg there despite the slickness.

With my pussy open to him and with my hand guiding his cock, he nudges my entrance. In one smooth motion, he shoves himself inside.

I cry out at the ribbed intrusion and painful stretch.

"Fuck," he hisses. He pulls out and roughly pushes back in. He does it again and again, each time a claiming of sorts.

The pain transforms to the intense pleasure of feeling so utterly full. Every inch of him and his piercings lights a fire to every sensitive spot within me, and it almost consumes me in a fiery inferno. I start to moan unintelligible words while he rocks within me, slamming in the last inch each time. Every nibble to my neck drives me further over the edge, and it's as though he knows what I want, when I need it. My breasts bounce with every pump, my nipples rubbing against his pecs. It only serves to heighten my arousal as he whispers things I'd never thought I'd like in my ear. Are they promises? Are they confessions?

When my moans become too loud for the rain, he takes my mouth again, and I whimper against his tongue.

By now, I'm soaked, both inside and outside. The weather doesn't relent, but I don't give a shit. Not in this moment. I don't care that I'm naked, getting fucked out in the open, getting owned by a scarred, tattooed, walking red flag.

My skin begins to heat, and the fire in my belly swirls once more as he takes me closer and closer to the edge of no return. I know I'll never see him again, but the way he handles my body, the intensity with which he can force me to feel…it's here and now that I know I'll be addicted to him for the rest of my life. He'll be a high I'll never be able to chase again, and I'll crave him until the day I die.

With one more deep and possessing stroke, I fall over the edge, moaning loudly in his mouth. My pussy clamps around him, milks him, and soon, he's joining me with the deep sounds of pleasure. My orgasm goes on and on, giving me no break, forcing me to take it all until he stills inside me, pulsing as he finds his release.

Breathless, we come down from our high and release each other's mouths. He slowly lowers my leg, pulling out of me and leaving a mess dripping between my thighs. Any normal person would be ashamed that they got fucked in a parking lot by a man who has the word "sinner" tattooed across his chest, but tonight, I feel no shame. Tonight, I feel everything else but shame. Greed. A whole lot of greed, because as much as I don't want to admit it, I'll dream about this encounter for eternity.

"You cheated," I say, grabbing my drenched shirt off the ground.

He bends to pick up his own clothes, and together, we try to slip into the fabrics.

"Hmm?" he asks.

"You didn't tell me something about yourself. Tell me something real. Anything."

"Why?" he asks, pausing in grabbing his pants.

Because I'm not done with you yet. Because I want just a tidbit about the man that will literally live in my dreams until I'm dead. Instead of saying those things, I shrug. "Humor me."

He lifts an eyebrow and then grins as if he has an inside joke he doesn't care to share with the world. "I'm the son of a cult leader, and I ran away to join the army so I could legally murder people."

I roll my eyes. "I meant a serious one. Not a made-up one."

With both of us fully clothed—at least enough to part ways, get in our cars, and drive home—he licks the raindrops off his lips with a smirk and says, "I'll leave you to ponder if I'm being serious or not."

And with that, he grabs the back of my neck, presses a rough kiss against my lips, bends to grab his knife, and abandons me in the rain. I stand there like a dumbstruck fool until he hops in his truck and the engine roars to life.

As he backs out, I turn to watch him leave, and dammit if he still isn't wearing that sexy, confident grin. It leaves me to wonder…how much of what he said was real, and how much of it was to make me more curious than I already am, knowing I'll never get the answers in the end anyway?

CHAPTER FIVE
JAGGER VALENTINE

THE SUN SHINES on my face, and the warmth from it makes sweat bead on my forehead. I'd like to think that that's the reason I stirred awake, but truth be told, I wasn't fully asleep anyway. It's been a long-ass time since I've slept properly, so long that I'm not even sure I ever have.

I rub my eyes with the heels of my palms and turn my head toward the alarm on the nightstand. Blue numbers glare back the morning's time: 8:03. I swear under my breath. I knew I'd be hungover this morning, knew that I'd have this pounding headache, but I had hoped I'd sleep until midafternoon to stave it off.

No such luck.

Whipping back my sheet, I gather myself to a sitting position and reach for the bottle of acetaminophen next to the alarm clock. The pills rattle around until a few fall into my waiting palm. I pop them into my mouth and grab the stale glass of water that was next to the bottle of medicine.

As soon as I swallow, I flop on my back on my pillow and groan at the texture of the ceiling. I remember last night clearly, remember that I got laid by some gorgeous woman in the parking lot. Was it reckless of me to have us fuck out in the open? Absolutely. Do I care any more about it this morning than I did last night? Not at all. I crave a good time, the distraction, and that's exactly what last night was. Screw the fact that she was stunning, and screw the fact that she made the most delicious noises as she came on my cock. It was just one night of drunken fun, and therefore, I have nothing to be ashamed of.

But she let me mark her. She let me claim her as mine for the night. My cock gets hard just thinking about it, and now I wish I'd played a little catch and release in the trees behind the bar until she couldn't run from me any longer. Then I would have fucked her in the forest like the animal I feel inside.

My phone starts to ring the moment I remember what her skin tasted like, and I grind my teeth together because not only did it ruin my daydream, but it's also making my head pound harder. Splaying out my hand, I search for it on my bed and find it tucked underneath a pillow. I bring it to my face and squint at the screen. It takes me a few seconds of contemplating if I want to answer his call so early in the morning or ignore him for a few more hours.

I press the green button, giving in to the pressure of the ring. "Yeah, man?"

"Morning, my Valentine sunshine," Blake says on the other end, his voice way too chipper for my current mood.

Blake Lowe, my best friend and fellow soldier who was in our unit. I'm not surprised he called. He does every morning, and if he's not at work, he'll call every night too. Sometimes he forgoes the phone and randomly shows up himself at one point throughout the day.

Blake owns a small security business, having started it as soon as we got back. He wanted to earn an income with the skills he learned in battle, and since the options were limited, he started his own. Since Ashland is small, he only has a few clients and a few employees, but it's enough to earn a decent living.

Sometimes—not very often—he employs me. Not that I need it. I know he's just giving me something to do on my particularly rough days. The things I did overseas paid me so well that I have some time before I actually have to go searching for a job. Truth be told, I don't know if I'll ever be behind a desk. I'll probably take Blake up on his offer and work for him permanently, but I just don't want to be more under his watchful eyes than I already am.

"You're too happy in the mornings," I murmur as I scoot myself up into a seated position once again.

"If you were a normal person, you'd get up at a normal time and be happy about it too."

I roll my eyes, even though I know he can't see me.

His voice grows more somber. "What time did you get in last night?"

"I didn't go anywhere," I immediately lie. He's been on my case ever since he got over his own demons and stopped drinking with me and mine.

"You're such a damn liar. I just happened to be driving by your apartment last night, and your truck was nowhere in sight."

I clench my jaw for a second. "Must have been when I was at the gas station."

"Right." I can tell by his tone that he knows I'm full of shit.

Standing on my feet, I stretch one arm above my head, walk around my bed, and exit my room into the shadowed hallway. "I dream of the day that you don't keep tabs on me."

He chuffs. "Someone has to."

"Sure."

"I'm the only one you got."

"I don't need a mother." I had one momentarily. She died and left me with my father.

His voice quiets. "If I don't watch over you, who will, Jag?"

Although I don't like it, he's right. I have no family, not anymore. No friends, no one who tolerates me. It's just me and Blake.

I pinch the bridge of my nose as I step foot into the dark kitchen and halt in my step just before the cabinet that has my precious cereal inside. Blake makes fun of me and my cereal, calling me a child, but honestly, I was never allowed to eat it as a child and spent most of my adult life in places that didn't have cereal—not like America's. I just tell him to fuck off between each bite.

"God," I answer.

"God is the one who gave you life, dumbass. I'm the one keeping you alive, but you're damn determined to see him before your time."

"You act like I'm suicidal," I grumble deeply, reaching for my cereal, pulling it down, and digging my hand inside for that frosted goodness.

"In a way, you are."

Chewing thoughtfully, I finally say around the mouthful, "Is this why you called?"

"Isn't it why I call every morning? I have to make sure you're still breathing."

"Well, I appreciate it," I say honestly, digging around inside the box for another handful. I truly mean it.

As soon as the words are out of my mouth, there's a knock at my door. I whip my head that direction and scowl. The only person who has ever knocked at my door is Blake, and he's on the phone.

"Is someone at your door?" Blake asks incredulously.

"Yeah," I mutter.

The knock comes again.

"You gonna answer it?" There's humor in his tone because we both know that there's a good chance it's a cop on the other side. For what, I don't know, but I wouldn't be surprised.

I set the box down and head toward the door in the living room. It's only a few feet, and I gobble the steps up in no time. I grab the door handle, swing it open, and swallow my next breath with difficulty.

"Hi," she greets, that beauty from last night, the woman I had pinned against my truck. She stands there all gorgeous, hair silky straight and body wrapped in comfortable business attire. It makes me self-conscious about how I'm dressed. I'm sure my hair is sticking up in many directions, I'm shirtless, and I'm not wearing any briefs under my gray sweatpants.

"Who is it?" Blake asks, fully curious now that I haven't said a single word.

"I gotta go," I say to Blake, and then I hang up immediately. To Dolly, I rumble, "How did you find me?" It's a question I'd really like to know. Did she follow me home? Is she a stalker? Sure, we had fun last night. Sure, it was mindblowing, but when I leave, I don't expect to see them again.

She lifts an arm and holds up a wallet between pinched fingers. *My wallet.* "This fell out of your pants last night. I didn't notice it until after you were gone."

"How did you find me?" I ask again, dumbfounded, uncertain, and unsteady. I've never had anyone else in my space that didn't involve sex. At least, not when I was sober, not like this.

She scowls and glances at the wallet before shoving it in my direction. "Your driver's license."

I take it from her and murmur my thanks.

She peeks around my shoulder. "So this is where you live?" she questions, and I turn to glance with her. Empty bottles of beer and liquor are on every surface, and I could give two shits about it.

I don't bother to answer her. Clearly this is where I live.

She whistles low. "That's a lot of—um...I'm surprised you're not dead."

I turn back toward her and raise an eyebrow. "What? Are you a doctor or something?"

"Therapist actually," she says, beaming. That smile does something to my dark insides, a tiny ray of light, but it's gone as soon as her smile is.

"Right," I rumble deep, and I watch as she does a little shiver. I remember my voice having an effect on her last night, and it sends back all those memories. "I don't need one."

She laughs—actually laughs—and every muscle in my body locks up. "I beg to differ."

"And what makes you say that?" I ask, resting my arm on the door frame and leaning against it.

Her gaze sweeps the muscles in my tattooed arm, but I don't move because I want to hear her answer. She may be hot as hell, she may be a good fuck, but she's only known me for thirty minutes.

"I know a dark soul when I see one." She crosses her arms over her chest and glares at me, despite my posture having some sort of effect on her. "I know someone who is tortured on the inside as soon as they speak. You're a therapist's wet dream. I'd put my last dollar on it."

I don't like the fine points of this conversation, so I change its direction. "Is that why you're really here, darling?" I purr, lifting a hand and moving her hair gently over her shoulder. She holds her breath as I do, but I couldn't help the urge. I had to see if her hair felt as soft as it looked. It is. "To fix me?" I lower my voice as last night's memory slowly replays in my head. "Or are you here for another good time?"

I watch as she swallows with difficulty. A blush creeps up on her face. "I don't know what you're talking about."

"You could have left my wallet with the bartender."

"Didn't seem right."

I lean a little in her direction. "Fix me or fuck me? Which one is it, Dolly?"

Her eyes go back and forth between mine, searching for…what? My soul? My father took that a long time ago.

She glances down at my lips, lingers her gaze there, before she says, "I—I have to go."

"Mm-hmm," I hum as she backs away.

"I have a client soon."

"Mm-hmm," I hum again, watching as she heads toward the stairs. In a deep rumble, I add, "See you soon." Because I know she'll be back. I know an addict when I see one because I am one, and it just so happens that I've become her new fix. Normally I'd mind, but with her…

She doesn't look back at me as she takes the steps quickly, and I smirk as I head back inside my apartment, shut the door, and walk back to my breakfast.

She'll definitely be back.

I slap my wallet on the counter, and as soon as I do, a business card falls out. A quick glance tells me it's Dolly's and just what occupation she has. I take a deep breath and breathe out a curse word. Nothing pisses me off more than her getting the last word in the end, and in more ways than one.

CHAPTER SIX
DOLLY STERLING

SADIE'S FACE is hidden behind the bistro's giant menu when I arrive. I pull out the chair from the chipped and worn table and take a seat across from her. It's a chilly afternoon, but she had chosen an outdoor table anyway. I understand why. Most of Sadie's quirks have to do with having been confined her entire life. If she can sit outside in an unfamiliar place, she'd rather.

The sound of my chair's legs scraping against the concrete floor causes a few heads to tip my way, including Sadie's. She lowers her menu, but instead of her bright smile, she has a deep frown.

"Geez, I'm sorry I'm late!" I whisper-yell as I take a seat.

She lays the menu flat on the table and jabs it with a pointer finger. "I've been waiting for at least fifteen minutes, and you've ignored all my texts."

"I was driving."

I try to hide my smile, but I completely fail. She's such a control freak.

Sadie is as platinum blond as they come. She dyes it, and I know this because I've helped her spread the bleach near her dark roots a few times. Her makeup is always wildly dark, highlighting her baby-blue eyes while also masking the woman underneath. It's a purposeful act, the perfect disguise. Smoky eyeshadow, eyeliner, and black lipstick make her entire appearance complete.

To accent those, she has a pierced nostril, eyebrow, and lip, as well as tattoos on her hands. I suspect she has more tattoos, but she usually wears some sort of long-sleeve shirt and tight skinny jeans, so I never get to see them.

Sadie closes her eyes for a second. I wait for her to gather herself and pick up my menu, opening it to today's specials. She'll be fine once she takes a few deep breaths and remembers that she can't puppet the world so she's never caught unaware. She may not realize that's what she's doing, but I certainly do.

"How was your week?" I ask, changing the subject without looking at her to see if she's ready for a different topic.

"Had a few cool tattoos and a date. That's about it."

Sadie works at the town's only tattoo shop, and she could be one of the most sought-after artists in the area if she didn't hide herself behind the other men that work there.

I may not like that she hides behind the makeup and those closest to her and that she has the control issues and secrets from everyone but me, but I do know that it's for her safety, and therefore, I respect it. It's Sadie's past rearing its ugly head, and truth be told, I don't think she will ever be able to stop or change, even if the threat is no longer there anymore.

There was a time when she was so scared that she wore wigs. I finally talked her into just dyeing it.

When I first met Sadie, she was in an alley behind my office building. She was literally inside the dumpster searching for anything to help her survive the cold streets: food, clothes, money, or things she could trade with the other homeless or the pawn shop. I had the rest of the afternoon off, so I took her into my office, gave her somewhere warm to heat her fingers from the winter's chill, and fed her my lunch. She had eaten it so fast that I thought she was going to be sick, and once she was finished, I asked her if she needed help.

She wouldn't talk to me at first. In the beginning, after she had eaten, she had gotten up and looked at the pictures on my shelves and touched the spines of my books. Eventually, among the books and the pictures, she found reassurance and said, "I'm hiding," and that's where the conversation began.

Sadie is from a cult. I know it's a religious cult, one that believes in being pure and clean, but to this day, I don't know much about it. She doesn't want to talk about it, refuses to discuss what happened there and how she escaped. I do know that the cult lives on one property, a compound of sorts where the leader can keep tabs on his "flock." And once you're in it, you're in it for life. There is no escape, and if you do, you're sacrificed in a ritual to cleanse the souls of all those within the cult, or worse, forced to survive your punishment.

So we came up with a plan. I helped her get a place to live and gave her money to do so and to fill her fridge with groceries until she scored the job at the tattoo shop. She had a gift in art, and they saw it right away, just like I did. I helped her become someone else entirely, and quickly we became best friends, despite the fact that she's half a decade younger than my thirty years. Even though we look nothing alike, I consider her my sister.

She looks up and raises an eyebrow at me. "When are you going to let me tattoo you? Or one of the guys could. They're all single, you know."

"Stop trying to hook me up with them," I say, rolling my eyes. They're attractive, but they're just not my type. Though they're covered in tattoos and I'm attracted to tattoos, they're too sweet. For the life of me, I cannot make myself love someone who is nice. I'm doomed to date what my mother would consider a red flag.

My mind drifts back to Jagger and what we did together in the rain a few days ago. I don't regret it. I don't even regret showing up at his place. The look on his face was entirely worth it. I know where he lives, and though that feels stalker-ish, I don't want to be done with him yet, even though common sense says to leave him alone.

He's trouble, but that last encounter we had at his apartment, I know he felt that connection too.

My heart sinks. I could have imagined the connection. It could have been all of the alcohol that fed me lies and cues that were there but not actually honest. God, I hope I didn't just make that up in my head because then I *will* look like a stalker, and I'll be chasing after some bad boy who will kick me to the curb the next time he sees me while sober.

Sadie cocks her head to the side. "Where'd you just go?"

"Nowhere." My dismay must have been showing on my face, and I quickly turn my expression neutral.

The waitress steps up to our table and takes our order, giving me a break from Sadie's curious stare while I gather my thoughts on what to tell her and even how much to tell her, because I know she's not going to drop this until she has some answers. She knows me too well, and I know her too well too. I know for a fact that she's not going to like what happened the other night, and that's the very reason that I haven't told her yet.

As soon as the waitress leaves with our order scribbled on her pad of paper, Sadie leans against the table and, in a hushed voice, says, "Spill, Dolly."

I cringe. "Do I have to?"

"Yes. I'm your bestie. I automatically deserve answers." She wrinkles her nose. "Unless it's disgusting, then I'd rather not know."

The waitress sets our glasses of water down, then straws, and disappears back into the restaurant without a single word. I pick up my straw, remove the wrapper, and start tying it in knots while twisting my lips to the side. Should I lie my ass off? Or do I give her the truth?

"Spill," she whispers again, this time with all the support of a true best friend in her tone.

The truth it is, because how could I not?

"So that guy the other night?"

Her eyes sparkle for the incoming gossip. "The hottie at the bar?"

I nod. "He came to sit at my table, remember?"

She smiles. "Did you get his number?"

I cringe. "No. No, not exactly."

"So…what? You just talked?" she asks, frowning.

I scratch the back of my head, the skin suddenly itchy there. Stabbing my straw into the ice of my water cup, I tell her the truth. "*Oh god,*" I begin in a whispering moan for the impending shit I'm going to get for this. "We had sex outside by his truck."

The frown smooths into a shocked expression, and she blinks a few times at me as the knowledge sinks in that I just had a one-night stand with a person I've never met and what kind of man that would make him.

She runs her tongue over her front teeth, not pleased at all with this news. "You told me you were done with the bad boys."

I cringe again and look away from her piercing stare. "I guess I'm not."

Out of the corner of my eye, I see her run a hand through her hair while pinching her eyes closed.

"Did you at least get his name?"

I look down at the table. "Jagger."

"Well, that's a start," she breathes out. "Are you going to see him again?"

Sliding my gaze back to her, I admit, "I did the following morning."

She shakes her head. "What did you do, Dolly?"

My cheeks tug as I pinch my lips together in annoyance. As a therapist, I don't mind finding other people's shortcomings, but when mine are pointed out, I tend to get a little sour. "I don't know what you're talking about."

"I know you," she hisses, leaning into the table again. "You cannot help yourself to prove a point, so what point did you prove, and why did you do it?"

My bottom teeth show in yet again, another cringe. "I found his wallet on the ground and took it to his place."

"Oh my god," she whispers. She lifts her hand and covers her mouth. Through her fingers, she adds, "You wanted him to know you were interested in more than just sex, didn't you?"

I scrub my face. "Yes. God, I'm an idiot."

She laughs out loud, and I drop my hands back to my lap, scowling at her finding humor in my issues. "You say I'm the control freak in this relationship, but have you ever looked at yourself?"

"I'm not a control freak," I counter. She's the controlling one. Right?

"You totally are. You wanted him to know you could find him whenever you wanted. Tell me, Dolly: did that conversation go well? Because bad boys with one-night stands tend to not like being found."

"Okay, so it didn't go well. We fought, but honestly, the fight was kinda fun. At least for me, and watching him squirm was probably the best part of it all."

"You know, for a therapist, you can be relentless." She pinches her fingers together. "And maybe a little evil."

"I never said I was perfect," I say, straightening my blouse. "I like him, and I want to know more about him."

"What? To see if there's something there?"

I shrug a little. "Maybe."

She points at me. "Let me tell you what's there."

"Oh god, here we go." I inhale slowly to calm the anger rising.

"Nothing but heartache, girl. Nothing but pain. He'll cut you so deep, just like all the others you become fascinated with, the ones you've tried to fix."

"But I do eventually fix them."

"And then they leave you, or you get bored and leave them. What happens if this one is unfixable? Because honestly, Dolly, who fucks someone outside of their truck and not inside of it? That's someone who is messed up in the head, causing them to be fearless with nothing to lose. You want to involve yourself with someone like that?"

I scowl at her again. "Hey, I'm the therapist here."

"And yet you didn't really consider that, did you? That this might be the one you cannot fix?"

"Everyone is fixable."

Something passes over her eyes, and I know I just sent her into her past. Quietly, she mutters, "No. No, they're not. Some people are too far gone."

The waitress brings our food, and we grow silent as we eat, contemplating all that we've discussed and leaving the conversation on the edge. I know that I brought up something with Sadie that was better left buried, and I also know that she needs to dwell on it, sit in it for a bit, because I know that avoiding something we've endured can cause worse damage than confronting it.

As for Jag? Well, that's something I'll have to sit on and sit with too. At least for a while until I figure out what to do. Hell, maybe I can talk myself into forgetting him entirely.

CHAPTER SEVEN
JAGGER VALENTINE

THERE'S *a woman with dark brown eyes and wrinkles lining her forehead, and there's my gun raised by my firm hand. My finger pulls the trigger, and it fires, and then there's a bullet hole between her eyes.*

A man. He's short with dark hair, skin shades lighter than my hand held out before me, gun poised. The gun fires. His body thudding to the ground is louder, more impactful, than the gun itself.

A home ablaze. There are screams of the people burning alive inside while I peer at the box of matches digging into my palm.

An old man in a wooden chair. His limbs are tied. The knife in my hand lowers, and then I thrust forward right into the man's gut.

Blood. There's blood everywhere. In my fingernails, coating my palms, droplets running along my arms.

I jolt awake inside my dark room with nothing to give me light except the full moon shining through my bare window. My breathing is so out of control that it's coming out in short pants, and sweat coats my skin in a fine sheen.

Searching my room wildly, it takes me a minute to not see their faces, all those lives I've ended. All those people that don't exist anymore because of me. It took nothing to kill them. No second thoughts, no hesitation, no questions asked. I did what I was told. I was a good soldier.

And now?

Now look at me.

Now I dream about them. *Now* my soul wonders what the fuck I did and if it was truly worth being just as dead inside. If running from my past was worth being this… monster; a trade of one evil for another.

Often, I'm curious if their deaths will eventually, and truly, end me. If it'll eat me alive. If it will consume everything that I have left. If it will change me so far away from the man I want to be that there won't be a sliver of hope left.

I run a hand through my slick hair and work like hell to get my breath under control. It takes a few minutes, my hand over my heart, to calm the heavy beats. Eventually, it works. The feeling of what I had done doesn't go away, but the reality sets in that I'm not there anymore. That I'm home, in my country, in my apartment, in my bed.

This is my pillow I ordered. These are my black walls that I painted. Those are my shoes that I was convinced to buy. That's my wallet that Darling returned a few days ago.

Dolly. *Darling.*

She was real. She wasn't a dream. She was a living, breathing thing. Someone I hadn't killed, someone who had sought me out instead of someone I hunted.

I cannot convince the pain in my soul to dissipate, so I do the only thing I can do. I grab the vodka off the floor and take a big swig. And another. And another. I then set it back down on the floor and stand. I pay no mind to the burn in my throat as I head toward the hallway and to the bathroom across from my bedroom.

My shower is cold because I don't wait for it to heat. I

don't deserve comfort, and truth be told, a cold shower creates discipline, which is what I need most right now.

By the time I'm done showering, I feel marginally more like myself, at least the parts of me that are left. I step out of the shower, grab my towel, and wrap it around my waist. Steam billows around me as I exit the bathroom, only to stop short.

Blake leans against the hall wall, and his arms are crossed over his chest with a blank expression on his face. He's wearing his jean jacket with sweatpants, as if he had just decided on a whim to come to my home and check on me. Hell, maybe I have some missed calls from him, and he was worried.

"Hey," I grumble as I cross the hall and back into my room. I try not to be annoyed with him for treating me like his personal patient, but it seeps through my voice anyway. "What's up, man?"

I can hear his quiet chuff, and he follows me partway into my room, his arms still crossed. His expression is no longer void but full of as much annoyance as what's inside me. I'm sure he's frustrated for similar reasons, but he really needs to understand that I can take care of myself, that I can endure this by myself. I don't want to lose him as my best friend—as my only family—but he needs to realize that I don't need anyone and shouldn't need anyone. I can survive on my own without bringing anyone else down with me. I did it my entire childhood, surrounded by the worst kind of people. I survived. I survived wars. I survived battle. I survived poverty. And I can survive the aftermath of what's left of me. There's no way in hell I'm going to take Blake's life from him.

"I came by last night."

My stomach knots for a second. "Did you?"

"You didn't answer the door."

"I was grocery shopping," I lie, bending and searching through a clean basket of clothes.

"The grocery stores aren't open that late. Stop lying, Jag. You were at the bar."

I briefly close my eyes and then turn a hard look in his direction. "And if I was?"

He flexes his jaw for a second, taking me in, searching me for some part of me that's familiar to him. And then his gaze lands on the vodka on my floor and the puddle flowing around it. *I forgot to put the cap back on.*

He raises his gaze to mine, and if looks could kill, I'd be dead.

"You're ruining what's left of your life," he says so quietly that I almost don't hear him. "You're pure destruction to yourself and to those around you."

I know, I want to tell him.

"Then why are you still here?" I demand just as softly, straightening my spine with a pair of black jeans in my hand.

He steps further into my room. For a second, as his courage takes up too much space, the room feels too small, and claustrophobia grips me.

"Because I won't leave my best friend behind."

"Let me disappear, Blake."

"No."

"Yes!" I yell, my voice ringing throughout the room. I toss the shorts on the bed with force, but he doesn't flinch at my act of aggression.

"You spent your entire adulthood hiding, Jag." He keeps his tone calm and even. "First from the place you ran from, and now from the army who abandoned you after they wrung you dry."

I open my arms wide, encompassing the world. "What's done is done. Neither you nor I can change it or what I've become."

I watch his jaw flex for several seconds until he says, "I know what you're doing at night after the bar. You're going to that compound and watching. Waiting. What are your plans, Jag? Are you going to burn it down?"

"I've thought about it."

"With everyone inside?" he asks, eyebrow raised.

I've done it before, my dreams remember it well.

I place my hands on my hips and stiffen my posture. "Once I get my sister out, then I just might." Fuck them all. They can die for what they've put me through. But I wasn't alone in the trauma. My sister was right there with me, and she…she's still there, even after all these years. She never found a way to escape like I had. "Are you really going to try and stop me?"

He considers me for several more seconds. "No. No, I'd help you light the first match. But you're letting it swallow you. Pretty soon, there is going to be nothing left of you but just a shell. Just skin and bone, nothing inside. Is that what you want?"

"If that's what it takes to be normal again, then maybe. If that's what it takes to get my sister, then maybe. If that's what it takes to forget, then maybe."

He rakes a hand down his face. "I'd rather you be dead, man."

I lift my chin and swallow the rock that suddenly surfaces in my throat. "If that's what it takes to be free, then maybe."

He shakes his head. Both he and I know I'm not suicidal, but he gets my point, and truth be told, I get his.

In a blink, he stirs to action. He crosses the room and grabs my shoulders, tugging me into his embrace. "Fight, asshole," he murmurs next to my ear. "See someone if you have to, find a therapist and talk it out. If you can't be the old you, become a new you. Fight."

And then he lets me go, exits my room, and within a

few more seconds, my front door closes. I have two choices: I can either listen to him and call the only therapist I happen to know—Dolly—or I can continue with the therapist I've been seeing—alcohol. It's not an easy choice, and I know whatever I choose will officially seal my fate.

CHAPTER EIGHT
DOLLY STERLING

"YOU KNOW, you'd think he'd be timely since he set up this appointment himself," I mumble to the squirrel nearby. It's been bravely foraging the city park's grassy floor not too far from me. The rodent doesn't even spare me a glance. It's as if I'm nothing but a statue.

More like an idiot statue. An idiot for believing he'd come.

A breeze drifts by, ruffling my dress. I huff out a breath, pull my jacket tighter around me, and get a good look at my surroundings. This park has a playground, but there are no kids roughhousing on it at this time of morning. There are no sounds but the common wildlife.

On three sides, the playground is surrounded by trees, which hold a few trails for hiking. Every chance I get, I take leisurely strolls on those trails, finding peace in nature as much as I can because, believe it or not, my job isn't easy. People's emotions affect my own, and I need a place to gather myself and recenter.

I chose this place to meet him. He was determined to not be in my office, and although that's inconvenient, I understand. Men's mental health is a crisis the human race is facing, and most of them refuse to seek help. If this makes him more comfortable, I'm willing to do it.

Sadie's words filter back into my head, the ones

where she mentioned I'd want to try and fix him and that maybe he may not be fixable. I was excited when he called, eager to be in his space once more like the pathetic creep that I am, but I'm also curious to see if she's wrong.

I sit down a little roughly on the bench, wondering if I've truly become some kind of stalker for all the emotions and ridiculous reasonings I have for wanting to get together with him. I sit there for several minutes, coming up with scenarios and not giving a shit anymore that I may be centering my professional help around seeing him as much as possible.

God, I truly am pathetic.

I glance at my phone for the fifteenth time, realizing he is now a half hour late. "Definitely not coming," I grumble to myself and rise to my feet, dusting my ass off from the wooden bench's loose paint chips.

As I turn, I nearly jolt out of my skin. Standing just behind the bench is Jagger. He has his arms crossed over his chest, and even through the loose-fitting zip-up sweater, I can see his muscles bunch with stiffness. His gaze is swiveling around us.

Curious, I ask him, "What are you looking for?"

"Other people," he murmurs, and when he's satisfied that there are none, he turns his gaze to me. His expression is hard, as if he wants nothing to do with what he came here for, but the fact that he's here means some part of him knows he needs to be.

"What's wrong with other people?" My frown is deep.

"I don't want to be overheard. It's amazing to me that people don't realize who really runs this town. Whose fingers are gripping the necks of those who are deemed important and influential."

"And you don't want them to know anything about

you," I say slowly. I gesture to the bench, inviting him to sit, and say, "Why don't you tell me?"

His eyes narrow. "Don't."

I cock my head to the side, thoroughly confused now. "What?"

"This isn't a shrink-slash-patient thing. You're going to talk to me like you talked to me the other night, and if I feel like you're analyzing me, even a little bit, we are done."

Shit, I think to myself. He's going to be harder to emotionally reach than I thought if he's this resistant to help.

I shrug, pretending indifference. "Fine with me. How about we see what's on that trail? Have you ever been?"

He doesn't even say a word as he starts marching in the direction of the nearest marked path. I stand there dumbfounded, wondering how the hell I'm going to reach this guy, let alone get to know him better. A closed book doesn't begin to cover it. He's more like a sealed vault.

"Okay then," I whisper. Turning on a heel, I follow him.

It takes less than a minute for me to catch up with him and a few seconds more for the Oregon woods to swallow us whole. As soon as we're in their shadows, I start humming a small tune to ease my inner anxiety.

The chirping birds are louder here, and they dance from tree to tree. Trying to remain as open and carefree and easy-going as I can, I walk with my head swiveling every direction they go. "Do you like birds?" I ask.

"No," he immediately answers in that deep voice of his. I'm not going to lie, that tone does something for me, and I try like hell to not let it affect me in all the positive ways.

I notice that he's still stomping his way around, and

I'd be a fool if I missed the smell of beer on his skin. His hair is still damp, so I know he showered. The alcohol is seeping through his pores.

If I had questions about his drinking and erratic behavior before, I don't anymore. It's clear he has a problem with alcohol.

"Then what do you like?"

He turns toward me, and for a split second, the corner of his lips tips into a smirk. "Women."

My cheeks blush, knowing I happen to be one of those women. But then my stomach flip-flops because I'd be a fool to deny that I want to be his one woman.

I look down and let the toe of my flats kick a tiny twig out of the way. "That can't be all. What else?"

"I live a simple life, darling," he murmurs deeply. "What makes you think there's anything else?"

"That's not much of a life," I whisper back to him. "I like to sing. And be outside. And I take self-defense classes. Well, kind of. I have a friend teaching me self-defense, I don't know if you can count that as a class or not, but—"

He looks me up and down. "You ramble when you're nervous."

I run a hand through my hair, having been caught at one of my faults. "Um. Yes."

He stops in his tracks, and I turn to face him, scowling in his direction. I open my mouth to ask him if he's already ready to go back, but he takes a step in my direction. That smirk is back on his face, and I back away from him. He continues to stalk toward me, all the way until my spine hits a cedar tree trunk. The bark bites into my skin through my jacket while his warmth seeps through the fabric because he's that close.

"Do I make you nervous, Dolly darling?" *God, that voice.* So bass-y. So sexy.

I can't help it; my bottom lip tucks between my teeth, and my eyes roam his cheeks for fear of looking in his eyes and seeing what rests there. I know if I look, I'll get a glimpse of his soul, and I don't know if I should like what I'll find.

He lifts his hand and gently, teasingly, tugs my bottom lip out of my teeth, then runs his thumb over it. "Answer me," he whispers so low that I almost can't understand him.

"Yes," I breathe.

Using the crook of his index finger, he lifts my chin, forcing me to meet his gaze. As soon as I do, butterflies explode in my stomach. *Sweet Jesus, I'm a goner.* His irises are so dark that they sparkle with all the demons he holds inside. So dark, they're just like a predator's. And me? I'm the prey. I know it, right in this moment, that I'm the prey, and right this second, he has his eyes set on me.

It explains everything from the other night and his act of claiming me, of forcing me to remember him by the mark on my skin and the scar it might cause.

It *thrills* me. It *scares* me more because I can tell he's done shit. Shit that feeds his inner demons. Shit that causes him to drink to forget. Shit that makes him seek women just for a few minutes of comfort—the only kind of comfort he'll accept.

But in this moment, the true reason I'm scared is the fact that a hunter is touching me, is gazing into my eyes, daring me to scream, to run, to hide, because no one is around and he can do whatever he wants to me.

Goose bumps rise on my skin, and my feet beg to move.

"Run, Dolly darling."

Before I know it, I'm running. Not on the path. No, the idiot in me is running into the woods. I leap over fallen logs, making a mad dash for…anywhere.

Anywhere that can hide me. A boulder, a hollowed-out trunk. Anything. And if I had any question if he was following me, it's confirmed when I hear a deep chuckle behind me.

"What are you going to do when I catch you?"

I don't answer him and instead pump my legs faster and harder, the adrenaline dump of fear and delight both mixing under my skin. It's a confusing concoction, but I know I have to keep moving. I know I have to try harder.

"I've chased down faster men than you," he taunts, his tone fully predatory. "Run, run, run."

We reach a small clearing, and a sob rips from my throat, knowing that out in the open, I'm doomed. Within the next few seconds, arms wrap around my waist, and we're taken down into the tall grass.

He isn't even out of breath like I am when he bends his head to my ear and whispers, "I can smell your fear, and even though it's the most intoxicating thing, do you know what else I smell?"

I shake my head, and at the same time, my nipples harden, because against my ass, I feel his rock-hard cock. I remember exactly what that cock felt like.

"How much you want it," he answers as he rocks his hips into my ass.

I try to hide my moan, but he hears it anyway and chuckles in my ear. With exceptional strength and complete authority, he lifts himself slightly to flip me over underneath him.

His dark grin is the first thing I see, and then I look into his eyes and see those demons right on the surface. Adrenaline spikes once more, my skin heating impossibly hot because I know that this is a dangerous game, and he's a dangerous man.

"Such pretty tears," he murmurs. "And just for me," he adds, right before he roughly captures my mouth. I don't know why I do it. Perhaps I'm already fixated on him, or perhaps I'm a masochist, but I kiss him back with as much vigor. My kiss is almost excited, full of anticipation that's mixing with the salt of my tears, because even though this kind of intimacy screams a troubled soul, I fucking love it.

One of his hands snakes between us, and the button of his jeans is popped open. He grabs and angles my right knee, and my dress falls to my hips. With skill, he shoves my panties aside, lines himself up to me, and pushes in. I get no room to adjust to his size and no warning for the pain. I gasp into his mouth, and he slides his hand under my head with the arm whose elbow is supporting his weight. Roughly, he twines his fingers into the nape of my hair and tugs, forcing the angle of my head to tip up toward the sky.

His pumps are not lazy. They're not gentle either. They're rough, to the point where it's almost burning. I let the pain travel through me, fueling my arousal, because as much as I loved the chase, I also love the desperation. The *need* to have me. Those demons are indeed out to play, forcing his actions, especially as he leans into the crook of my neck and bites down so hard that I cry out.

The ache from my hair and the pain from my neck and my pussy nearly send me over the edge. I've had pain during sex before, and while I didn't really enjoy it, I didn't stop it. But this time? It feels like it means something more. Perhaps it's because I'm more intrigued by him and want him more than I've wanted anyone else in a long time, and perhaps that reason is because logically, I shouldn't want him at all.

I reach the edge of my climax in a hurry, digging my nails into his hips and tugging him toward me faster, begging him to quicken his pace. He growls against my skin, releases the bite, and licks at the bruise that is surely forming along my pale skin.

He doesn't deny me my request. His pumps become impossibly hard and swift, and I know I'm going to have trouble sitting for days. That thought alone sends me over the edge, and I throw my head back against his hand and let out a scream so loud that the birds stop singing for a second.

Letting go of my hair, he lifts himself up and watches me come undone beneath him. "Fucking fall apart, darling," I hear him mumble. He grabs both of my thick hips and tightens his grip, echoing the pain radiating everywhere else on my body. I continue to ride the waves of his cock shoving in and out of me so hard, so fast, that I can't even think straight.

As soon as I come down from the orgasm, he pulls out and flips me over. I barely register what's going on until my ass is in the air and my knees are digging into the dirt. I cry out at the sudden change and then gasp when he grasps both of my arms and holds them together at the wrists with his fingers.

And then he shoves inside so far that my moan of agony and pleasure is just about as deep as his voice. "There's more to you than I thought," he says in such a sexy tone that my pussy ripples around him. "You like this, don't you, darling? You want me to own you, fuck you until you can't breathe, and leave marks all over you like the delicate porcelain doll that you are."

I don't answer him, and when he realizes that I'm not going to, he grabs the back of my hair with his free hand and yanks my front half off the ground. "Answer me," he demands.

Tears spring to my eyes from the strain of the skin on my scalp. "Yes," I breathe out.

"Tell me more."

"I fucking love it," I whimper. "Please. Please, Jagger."

He squeezes my wrists tighter and then punctuates, "Please what?"

"Please."

"Say it."

"Make me come. Please."

He lowers my front half back to the ground and moves his hands to my hips, curls his fingers back into my curves, and buries his cock so deep, so fast, that it takes everything I can do to not collapse onto the grass from the force of it all.

His cock hits just the right spot over and over again, and I can feel that fire build in my stomach, swirling and curling and waiting for that moment that it'll tip over the edge and send me into oblivion.

"Do it," he demands, and against my will, my body obeys, and I'm screaming against the feathers of grass beneath my face.

"Shit," I hear him hiss as my pussy clamps around him so tight that he has a hard time pumping at the same pace.

In the next second, he yanks himself out. Warmth splashes against my ass as he comes against both ass cheeks, fully owning me in every possible way.

Our breathing is ragged, and while we both come down from the high, he slowly releases the tension in his body. I look behind me. Our eyes clash, and for the first time since I've met him, his demons aren't swirling within their depths. Dare I say it, he almost looks relieved.

I gather myself to my knees and turn to face him. This is the perfect opportunity for me to get to know him, now that his walls are lowered. "So this is the real you?"

He stands, pulls up his jeans, and says, "I don't lie about who I am," as he buttons them.

I chew on the inside of my lip but remain with my knees in the grass. "Do you not like who you are?"

And right then and there, I knew I said the wrong thing. Right then and there, I realized that this primal need of his is his way to escape himself, and I just brought what haunts him back to the surface after seconds of it being tucked away. But I also know that my question needs to be asked.

"Sounds like shrink questions."

I shake my head. "Just getting to know you."

He narrows his eyes. "Doesn't sound like a question that someone would normally ask."

Bravely, I press on without missing a beat. "Tell me about the military." I'd been curious about it the moment he mentioned it. After much thought, I decided to believe him when I previously thought that line was full of shit. I still don't know if what he was saying about the cult was true or just something he pulled out of his ass. I have some experience with the result of cult life thanks to Sadie, so if it is true, maybe I can help him with that too. If he'll let me.

His jaw immediately clamps, and he turns on his heel. "I'm done."

As he starts stomping away, I quickly jump to my feet and follow him, yanking up my underwear as I go. "Why? Why don't you want to talk about it?"

He doesn't spare me a glance even though I've caught up to him. "Stop."

"No." I'm not going to let him get away with not answering me, of not even trying to relieve some of his burden onto me. "Tell me about the cult."

His pace quickens, and I have to jog to keep up with him.

"You just chased me in the woods and fucked me until I saw God. Tell me, Jagger. Tell me something."

He stops, grabs my arms, and forces me to look at him. His grip is strong as he says, "I'm a monster. Do you understand? I will not change, and you cannot force me to change. I am who I am now, and there's not a single shred of who I'm supposed to be left. Do you understand? So either you enjoy my company and who I am, or you step aside and don't let me contact you again."

I lift an eyebrow. "Do you plan to contact me again?"

He glances once at my lips and then back into my eyes. "You're addicting to everything that's wrong with me. It'd be in your best interest to never let me near you again."

"Not going to happen," I admit right away. He may have sought me out for some reason unbeknownst to me, but I'm not going to let him back away from me so soon. Or ever, for that matter.

"Then you have a death wish."

And with that, he lets me go and leaves. This time, I don't follow him because I know that he's right. If I follow him, I'll beg, and if I do want to survive all things that are Jagger, I should really heed to his advice.

But I'm not going to. I'll let him have this win… for now.

CHAPTER NINE
JAGGER VALENTINE

I TAKE a sip of my beer as I sit in my truck outside the deceptively beautiful place I once called home. In the middle of the forest, just off of Ashland, is a compound. It's not gated, but the people inside are prisoners nonetheless. Or ignorant idiots.

I was a prisoner. Since the day I was born until the moment I cared more about my freedom than the cost of what it would take to have it and ran away.

Here, with the cedar trees towering over every house and building, is where my inner monster was born. Here, within the four walls of each of those buildings and homes, I suffered so greatly that it was worth the trade of one evil for another.

There are many small white-picket-fence-type homes on this twenty-five-acre property and several buildings that store things like the community vans and the food supply. There's a swing set somewhere in there—the only place I could escape when my sister and I were little. All of us kids met there, the ones that weren't devoted to our ways, the ones who knew better and dreamed bigger.

Savage Temple is what we—*they*—call them. A cult, a large group of individuals living on this property and following a way of life that's barbaric for the sake of the soul's purity.

And the cleansing? I remember every single one just as vividly as the first.

I was thirteen when I was forced to whip my sister. I remember the welts like it was yesterday: red, hot, some bleeding. It was a sick and twisted punishment for the both of us.

We had been in town on a small outing while I kept track and held the hand of my little sister, Isabelle. We were walking along the sidewalk with our escorting adults when a kind but dirty and homeless woman gave my sister a piece of candy. The head of the cult, Bryce, saw it and made me deliver the blows once we got back home because I didn't stop the lady when it happened. I didn't knock the candy out of my sister's hand because it came from an impure soul. I didn't make her spit it out when she popped it in her mouth. She was six.

The cult leader just happens to have my last name and share the same genes as me and my sister. *Our father*. What kind of dad is so detached that he has his one and only son nearly kill his one and only daughter over a piece of hardened sugar? Over the sake of being pure for God.

Issy is my everything, the only thing I've ever had to call my own, and she's the very reason I'm sitting here in the dark, inside my car, with a gun tucked in the waistband of my jeans. I have to find a way to save her. I've waited so long for this. I have to get her out, and if I have to fucking kill someone to do it, I will.

I pray the person I have to destroy is the man who helped bring me into this world. The cold barrel against my tailbone echoes it, begs for it. I've dreamed of that day since I was a child, and I could easily march onto the property and do so, but I'd never make it off alive. They wouldn't kill me outright. Or...they would attempt to make me pure again, and it's guaranteed to be the worst kind of hell I'd ever experience. Most likely they'd pull my sister into it. Most likely, they'd force me to watch while they did the most unimaginable things to her.

I'm not afraid of death. I'm not even afraid of pain. I'm afraid of what they'd do to her.

One of the buildings, the one that stores the vans, has some stirring inside it. Lights are being flicked on, and within a minute, the garage door is lifting.

I perk up in my seat, set down my beer in the cup holder, and hope like hell I'm far enough away and hidden to the point of not being seen. Slowly, the white van pulls out and creeps along the gravel driveway of the compound. Once it's on the road, I turn on my car and begin following from far behind.

My heart slams against my ribs. I don't know who is in it, I don't even know why I'm following it, but every instinct I have tells me I have to. This is how I ran away, when the elders were off getting groceries and doing other shopping, leaving us eighteen-year-olds to tend to the children. I and another bolted off the property and immediately separated in case one of us was caught. I never saw her again. I imagine she's dead because the only way I survived the hunger and stayed hidden was by signing up for the military.

The van pulls up to the grocery store and finds an empty spot in the parking lot, which isn't hard because at this time of night, the store is near closing and every other sensible person is tucked away in their home. But my father had the Temple shop at night to draw less attention. Some things must not have changed.

I park far enough away and tuck behind another truck so that I don't seem suspicious, and then I turn off the engine. In the dark, my shallow breathing now the only sound, I wait for those inside the van to get out. The driver door opens, and out walks the worst of the worst in Savage Temple: Tyron Watts.

Even when I was young, I knew exactly what Tyron was doing within the cult. He liked little girls and young women, and my father never stopped his crimes. He turned a blind eye to it. I fully believe it was the motivator for the teen that escaped with me to leave in the first place. She was his daughter, and I can only imagine what it was like inside their four walls. Like me, she didn't have a mother to stop her father.

I grind my teeth and turn my attention to the passenger door as it opens. Whoever is in the front passenger seat is someone of importance, and since I'm no longer in the cult, it could be someone entirely different than my father, who usually rode along. I don't know what I'll do if I see him. I don't know if I can stay seated in my truck, knowing he'll be just inside that building, within a bullet's reach.

But that's not who steps out.

The wind knocks out of my chest when Isabelle plants her delicate flats on the pavement, has an easy and graceful look around, and turns to shut the van's door. Questions filter through my head, because even though she's now eighteen and not the twelve-year-old I left behind, she clearly has a place of importance within Savage Temple.

Regret fills me, near crippling. I should have never left without her. I should have taken her with me, even though I knew then that I wouldn't have been able to care for her and her survival would have been ensured if she stayed.

But why is she in the front passenger seat? Why is she the only one going shopping with Tyron? What piece am

I missing here? Being in a closed space with that man, and alone nonetheless, doesn't bode well.

Anger ripples through me, mixing with the regret in a poisonous combination. As soon as they stride inside the grocery store, I cannot stop myself from getting out of my truck. I need to see what's happening. I need to understand.

Once I jog across the parking lot, I peek inside the giant grocery store windows to check and make sure I won't be caught by at least Tyron when I enter. No one is there but a clerk dusting the newspaper stands, so I slip inside the door and quietly work my way past the shopping carts and toward the produce aisle. They're at the other end. My sister is plucking up green peppers off the shelf, bagging them, and placing them in the cart while Tyron watches on—more like watches her ass—like the useless prick he is.

I pick up an apple from the far other side of the aisle and pretend to observe it while I'm really studying my sister and how much she's changed. Dark circles are under her eyes. When we were younger, her eyes alone could light up a room, they were so bright and full of innocence. But now? They're dull. Still the same shade, but dull and lifeless and full of things that are painful for me to imagine.

Her dark-blond hair matches my own, but where mine is straight, hers curls in waves. She's not as tall as I am, certainly having gotten her height from the woman who birthed and abandoned us through death. My father always says Issy looks like her, and though my memory of my mother is fuzzy, I had tried to ignore those statements for fear that I'd hate my sister as much as my mother. My mother died during Issy's birth, and I still blame my mother to this day for leaving us. Part of me knows no one can control when it's their time, but the other part of me fully believes she gave up on living to escape the man she married.

I follow them into the next aisle, gathering a few groceries in my hand so that I go completely ignored. And once we hit the next aisle, I hear Tyron excuse himself to the bathroom. Brave move, because it'd be easy for Issy to escape now. But Issy doesn't even try. She stands there examining the boxes of pasta like she lives an ordinary life.

Frustrated and still seething with anger and regret, I drop my shit in the nearest display basket and immediately approach her. She startles when I grab her shoulders, but I still turn her to face me. "Issy? What the hell is going on?"

Her scowl is deep as she searches my face for recognition. I know I look a little older, and my hairstyle is entirely different, but I'm still me, and thankfully, after a few seconds, it hits her.

"Jagger?" she whispers in awe, gripping our cult's religious cross that's dangling around her neck. I'd tossed mine at the first chance. "You're not dead? How are you alive?"

"No," I snarl, and I know just who told her I was. "I'm alive, but how isn't important right now. What the hell is going on? Why are you shopping alone with Tyron? Why haven't you bolted yet? Why are you standing here right now and not having run?"

She closes her eyes for a second and steps out of my grasp. "Things are the same, yet oh-so-different since you left, Jag."

"What do you mean?" I ask, looking in the direction of the bathroom. We aren't far off, and I'm in plain sight if Tyron comes back out. I know for a fact that he'll recognize me the moment he sees me. He was basically my father's right-hand man.

She opens her eyes, and they're filled with such sadness that my heart cracks. "Tyron is my husband."

I step back as if I'd been pushed in the chest. For a second, my heart jumps several beats. "What the hell are you talking about?" I growl.

"Father decides who we marry, and since he's sick, he wanted me to marry someone who could take over the Temple when he passes."

"He's sick?"

She nods. "Cancer."

There's a part of me that takes complete joy out of the fact that he's suffering. "Why didn't you tell him no when he told you to marry him? Why didn't you escape? Why didn't you run?"

"I couldn't tell him no, Jagger!" Her volume is quiet, but the anger in it is so abrupt that it catches me off guard. And then in the next second, in the next breath, she's calm. "You know that. You know what kind of punishment I would have had if I had. And I couldn't have escaped. They have cameras everywhere on the compound now, they'd know where I would have headed. And even if I said no, even if I survived Father's cleansing and escaped successfully, the ties that the Temple has with the town are outmatched for someone like me. Someone the Temple has their claws in would have turned me in the moment they saw me alone."

I glance away, focusing on the shelf pasta and feeling such shame that I hadn't dragged her from that compound with me before the cult had gotten smarter than an eighteen-year-old's will to survive.

"So what? Are you just going to stay? Live a life with someone like Tyron?" I look back at her because I want to see the truth in her expression as she answers me. "Take over a cult you shouldn't believe in?"

She places a hand on her lower belly, and I follow the

movement. It doesn't hit me what she's implying until she says, "I have a child to think about now, Jag. I may be in the middle of my first trimester, but I have to think about him or her. I can't just leave and pray that they won't find me. I have someone else to think about now."

I clench my jaw. "And you think it's in the best interest of the child to stay? Who is the father, Issy?"

She looks at the bathroom and confirms my suspicion. I try not to let bile rise in my throat, both because I know my sister probably did not consent and second, because I know the hell her child will go through living under his roof.

"Come with me." I grab her elbow, begging. "Come with me now, and I'll take you far from here."

We both glance toward the bathroom when we hear the toilet flush on the other side of the door. "I can't." She rips her arm out of my grasp. "It's too late for me, but you can. You can still leave here without anyone knowing."

My nostrils flare. "Not without you."

She shoves me in the stomach. "Go!" she whispers. Her tone and expression are dripping in that same anger she displayed seconds ago. I don't recognize it. My sister never once had an angry bone in her body, and now… "Leave! If you're caught, you know what will happen to the both of us!"

My skin flares with heat. I know exactly what Father will do to her just to punish me, and then what he will do to me to punish her. Just because we haven't seen each other in many years doesn't mean we still don't love each other the same. The plea in her eyes tells me as much.

I start to back away. "I'll come for you."

"No, you won't," she begs with a sad tone. "Forget about me. Get far away from here and forget I exist."

I shake my head. "I will come for you, Issy. Mark my

words and believe when I say, your life won't end in that compound."

And then I turn on my heel and leave just as I hear the bathroom door open. I march right out of that grocery store fully believing that I will keep my promise, even if I don't know how yet.

CHAPTER TEN
DOLLY STERLING

EARLY IN THE MORNING, with my foam coffee cup in hand, I sit by the window in my favorite coffee shop downtown. Rollo and Sadie are in line, waiting for their own brewed deliciousness. They were both late, like usual, but I can't really blame them. Both have jobs that tend to go into the night hours.

While I waited for them to show up, I skimmed the paper sprawled out on the table. My mind was too muddled to continue to read the boring stuff happening in our town, though, so instead, I turned toward the window. I watch as the leaves rustle by and people stride to their destinations. I let the noises fall over me, the sound of the coffee grinder and the baristas' laughter and the chatter from the sleepy customers. My mind can't get off of what happened yesterday in the woods.

A van parked out front catches my eye for a split second. I can't see inside very well, but I can tell a woman is driving it based on the silhouette. The van tickles the back of my brain, and for a moment, I realize I saw it this morning parked down the street from my house. What a coincidence that we both started our morning at the same place.

It doesn't take long for Rollo to sit down beside me and nudge me with his shoulder.

"What's so interesting out there?"

His friendly voice is enough to pull my attention from outside. "Absolutely nothing."

"Then where did you go?" he asks while tapping his temple, letting me know he's fully aware that my mind isn't in the right place.

I scowl when I look at him. "None of your business."

He chuckles and shakes his head. "Who is he?"

"I have no idea what you're talking about."

I lift up the coffee mug and bring it to my lips to avoid his know-it-all gaze, but he gently snatches it out of my hand. If it weren't for the lid, it would have splashed all over me.

"I know you way too well, Dolly," he begins. "Your mind is on someone you met and someone you can't get out of your head. My only question is: is this guy worth it or not? Or is he another project you're falling for?"

"I don't fall for my projects," I lie through my teeth with an eye roll to go with it.

As he starts naming all the men I fell for, sort of fixed, and then they broke my heart, I start to cringe. By the time he's done, my expression is one of pain.

"And when it's all over, Sadie and I are left to pick up the pieces."

"What?" I grumble, finally glancing at him. "Am I a burden to you or something?" I don't know why I'm suddenly blaming him, but the topic isn't one I like to have with him because I truly care what he thinks. I never take his advice, though, because the heart wants what the heart wants, and what he suggests always goes against the heart. It's a stupid organ to listen to, but here I am, apparently repeating history time and time again.

He scowls at me. After a few minutes of studying my face, he murmurs, "Dolly, what's wrong?"

I gently take the coffee back from him and gulp a hot

sip just to feel something other than shame lodge in my throat. "He's…different than the others."

Sadie sits down, and having caught the last thing I said, she sighs loudly. "Don't tell me you saw him again."

"Wait, you know about this guy?" Rollo asks.

She nods but keeps her attention on me, waiting for my answer.

"Yes, okay? Yes, I saw him again."

"And? What happened?" Sadie grumbles, but they both lean in closer to get the gossip.

I pinch the bridge of my nose. Over my dead body am I going to tell them that he hunted me in the woods and fucked me among the sticks. They'd think I'm crazier than he is for wanting it to happen again. There's no way I'd be able to keep that off my face—the desire. They both know me too well.

"We talked for a little bit before it became too much for him."

"Well, you're a shrink," Rollo says, leaning away to rest his back on the back of the chair. "It's hard to give up that instinct."

"Yeah, I noticed that yesterday."

"You do it to us sometimes too," Sadie admits, then brings the coffee up to her mouth and smiles before she sips.

I pucker my lips, but I don't deny it. "Sorry," I mumble, because what else am I supposed to say?

"Meh." She waves a dismissive hand at me. "We're used to it, but I imagine what's-his-name wasn't too happy with it."

"Jagger."

"That's his name?" Rollo's cop voice makes an appearance.

"Yeah, why?"

He shrugs, but I can tell he's bothered. "That's not a common name."

"I'm aware. Why?"

"I picked a Jagger up a few times for public intoxication."

"And?" Sadie pipes in, completely interested. "What's your opinion?"

Rollo scratches his chin, the stubble he forgot to shave, and he looks every bit the cop that he is. "He has some problems. Big ones."

Sadie turns a glare at me. "I knew it."

"I can handle myself," I start in before they really get going. "He's not going to hurt me."

"Maybe not physically, but..." Rollo's voice trails off because, frankly, he doesn't need to finish the sentence.

"I'll keep my distance," I lie. I know I won't be able to, not emotionally and certainly not physically. I'm one hundred percent hooked.

Sadie chuffs. "No, you won't."

Tired of this conversation, I stand with my coffee and push my chair back. "I'm going to be late for work." She frowns as she watches me back away from the table. "I'll talk to you guys later." And then I turn and stride straight out of the coffee shop.

The brisk fall breeze breaks around me, making my hair flutter across my face and my dress ruffle at my thighs. I stomp in the direction of my car, murmuring about how pissed off I am.

Just as I get to my car and yank open the door, a familiar arm crosses my path and stops me from entering. I look up at Rollo and pin him with a glare.

"We're just worried, Dolly," he says, so quiet that it's barely audible above the wind.

"Well, you don't need to be."

"Look," he says, taking his arm out of my way and

using that hand to run through his hair. "The urge to find this guy and tell him to back off is strong. When I put him into the system…Dolly, there was a lot on his record and stuff about his past that I wasn't cleared to read. This could possibly be the worst guy you've picked up before."

"Maybe, but everyone deserves someone, and who better than someone who can help them?"

He gives me a sympathetic look because we both know I'm not going to take the advice he gives next. "That doesn't have to be your job if you don't want it to be. There are plenty of other women who could help him."

"Rollo," I grind out. "It's really none of your business. I stopped being your business when we signed divorce papers."

He laughs out loud. "You will always be my business. Just because we aren't married doesn't mean I don't care about what happens to you. You and Sadie are my closest friends. I'm going to watch out for you two whether you like it or not."

I sigh out loud, knowing he's just trying to be there for me, to watch out for me. "How about this? I promise to let you know when I'm in too deep."

He studies my face for a minute just to see if I'm being truthful and sincere, then he nods, satisfied. "I'll take what I can get."

I give him a smile that I don't mean and start to climb into the driver seat.

Leaning down, he adds, "You know the warning signs, Dolly. You know when someone is too far gone. Don't kid yourself if he happens to be one of them."

"Okay," I mutter, and with that, he shuts my door and heads back into the coffee shop.

I blow out a breath and start my car. My mind reels

the entire way to my office, going over every ounce of facts that have happened in the last twenty-four hours and how many questions I can possibly get answered in the next twenty-four.

As I pull up to my small red-bricked office, I squint my eyes because someone is waiting in front of it. I park the car, and my heart hammers in my chest. The man who is sitting on the second step has his hood up over his head, but I know exactly who it is. I practically have his body shape memorized at this point.

Jagger.

After getting out of the car, I slowly approach him. This close to a shrink's office has to be tough for him, and I don't want to spook him any more than he probably already is.

"What are you doing here?" I ask when I'm directly beside him. I take a seat on the step when he doesn't tip his head up to look at me.

Instead of answering me, he says, "I did a lot of tours, and every single one was worse than the last."

I lick my lips as my stomach does a few flip-flops. He's going to talk freely to me. I'd ask him to come inside, but I don't think he's ready for that. I think at the first glimpse of my couch, he'd run the opposite way. The fact that he's by the front door is a miracle.

"How so?"

He's stiff as he answers, "I was a monster, someone fucked up beyond repair before I went into the military, and they knew it as soon as I started training. I was immediately put on a special team, and that team was in charge of assassinations. I traded one evil for another, and they must have thought I could handle it. No one gets it, no one understands, but I think you might."

My heart sings that he thinks I can relate in some way,

but I'm not entirely sure what he's saying. I don't have the full picture yet. "What was the first evil?"

"My father." He didn't even hesitate to answer me.

"Tell me about him."

"No." He finally looks at me. "I'm not here to tell you about my fucked-up childhood. I'm simply here to tell you that there's no coming back from what they made me do, and there's no repairing what my father broke."

I place my hand on his knee. "There is if you let me help you."

"I don't need a shrink." I'm sure he hears how false that sounds as much as I do.

"Then how about a friend?"

He chuckles darkly, and his eyes smolder. The mood switch is incredible, but I also know it's a defense against his inner pain. "You and I both know we're past friendship."

CHAPTER ELEVEN
JAGGER VALENTINE

I'M NOT sure why I'm admitting all of this to her, but I do know that I feel more like who I'm supposed to be when I'm with her than when I'm alone. I don't even feel this little piece of normalcy when I'm with Blake, the guy who went through it all with me, the guy who has stood by my side as I fell apart afterward.

Her eyes swivel all over my face, and I don't know what she finds, but she eventually asks, "What is this, Jagger? What's happening between us?"

"I don't know, darling," I purr, a distraction because that question is one I'm not sure how to answer. Even if I tried to discover one, I'm not sure she'd like what I'd have to say. In the end, I know it wouldn't be enough for her. "You tell me."

"Don't," she says, scowling at me. "Don't try to change the subject by being sexy. Tell me something real. Answer what I've asked, or I'll go inside this building and the conversation will be over."

"And that's supposed to scare me?"

She raises an eyebrow in challenge. "You wouldn't be here if you didn't want a conversation with me."

I grind my teeth, knowing she's right. "What do you want from me? To tell you it's easier to breathe when you're around? That I want to make you understand because the feeling of finding some sort of meaning in life is a little easier when I can just simply smell you? Is that what you want to hear?"

She shrugs, but I can tell by the small blush on her cheeks that she's touched. She shouldn't be. She should heed them as warnings.

"Yes," she says.

"Why does it matter? Why can't we let this be whatever it is?"

She chuckles and shakes her head. "I know you're used to the one-night stands, but it turns out that I'm not that kind of woman."

I settle into a relaxed posture, happy to change the subject off of myself. "Then what kind are you?"

"I grew up with a decent family. I wasn't like you. My parents had me late in their lives, and they had their shit together because they waited. They were financially stable and had already gone through all the trials and errors as a couple. I grew up in a stable home with parents who were supportive, encouraging, and loving. I want nothing less for myself, but…"

"I'll never be a stable person," I whisper to her.

"That's why I said 'but,'" she whispers back. "I'm not attracted to those kinds of men, the ones who would bring about the stability that I was raised on."

"So you're attracted to those of us that are fucked up?"

"Essentially, yes." She grins a little, just the tips of the corners of her lips, which lets me know she's equally ashamed that she's attracted to my kind as well as encouraging me toward the fact that I shouldn't be ashamed there's a "my kind" to begin with.

"Where are your parents now?" I ask. I know that the moment I meet them, they'll snatch their daughter away so fast that she'll get whiplash.

Her smile disappears, and she turns her head to stare at the businesses across the street. "Dead. My mother passed from cancer a few years ago, and my father quickly followed her from a broken heart."

"I see," I mutter.

We're quiet for a moment, her staring off into space and me watching the side of her face, wishing that I could listen to her thoughts. Chances are they're gentler than mine, even if she's remembering loved ones that are dead. I know a thing or two about death, just not in the way she does.

Continuing to look forward, she asks, "Are you going to tell me about your parents?"

I clench my whole body on instinct. "Why are you obsessed with my past?"

She turns and looks at me, but instead of matching my hostility, her expression is open and honest. "I don't think you realize how much it's shaped your present and mapped out your future. Maybe, just maybe, telling someone about it will start some sort of healing that you're not capable of doing on your own. Who better to tell than someone who cares about you?"

I pinch the bridge of my nose, fighting every instinct to get up and walk away. But what if she's right? What if I seek her out because I know she could be that very person for me?

"My mother died when my sister was born. Some sort of complication," I begin, and she remains silent as I continue. "My father was a...leader for those we were closest to, and he often used my sister and me as examples of how everyone should act. He was equally religious and cruel, and somehow, in his mind, those went hand-in-hand."

He appears in the back of my mind, and my stomach turns over.

"So how did you get away from him?"

"I ran." I drop my hand to my side and then glance at her knees, focusing on the bare skin. Looking in her eyes would be too much right now, as shame is swirling in my gut, even though the shame shouldn't be mine. It should belong to the bastard who raised me. "When I was eighteen, I ran so fast and so far that he couldn't find me. I don't even think he knows if I'm alive or not. And as soon as I got to where I felt comfortable enough to pause, I joined the military, and they whisked me even further away."

"And your sister?" Her voice is so quiet, it's as though she's afraid to know the answer. She would be right in that fear.

"Still under his thumb." Finally, I meet her gaze. "She's in trouble. I have to save her. I just don't know how yet."

Her brows pinch together. "Is it something that the law can get involved in?"

I shake my head. "It doesn't work that way, trust me."

How can I possibly tell her that Savage Temple has their fingers in everything? Chances are, she's run into the cult and didn't even know it. If I tell her these things, she will not only feel an overwhelming amount of sympathy for me, which I don't want or need, but she'll start looking around, wondering who is involved in such evil. She's too innocent to be darkened by my past. The most I can do is shield her from the majority of it by keeping it to myself. I'll give her just enough to allow me into her space, but not enough to scare her.

She touches my knee. "You'll find a way."

The touch is so gentle that it's all I can focus on. No one has ever touched me like that, and frankly, I don't know what to make of it. I've certainly never touched someone so gingerly, so emotionally, and it makes me wonder one thing. "How come you aren't afraid of me after I chased you down? How come you weren't afraid of me then either?"

Taken aback by my sudden change in topic, she raises her eyebrows into her forehead. When the surprise of it settles, she admits, "I've been asking myself the same question since it happened. All I know is that I liked it, that even though you could hurt me, even kill me, I knew you wouldn't. At least...I hoped you wouldn't. But not knowing for sure just..."

I smirk. "It turned you on."

She blows out a breath. "Yeah. Yeah, it did."

"You do realize that that's who I am, right? That there are parts of me that will never mold to what other people consider normal and sane?"

She gives me another one of those small smiles and tucks a loose strand of hair behind her ear. "I think I'd get bored of you if you did."

I swap my gaze between her eyes and her lips, wanting nothing more than to devour and own the innocence that is Dolly. I want to hunt that part of her too. Instead, I refrain. For now, at least. "I wonder how someone with a simple and loving past ended up wanting the villain?"

"I ask myself that every day," she says with a laugh. "Even as a shrink, I do not have any answers. Perhaps it's because I seek adventure. Perhaps it's because I have tendencies to buck against my perfect, ordinary childhood. Your guess would be as good as mine."

I give in a little to my urges and reach for the back of her neck. Carefully, with as much restraint as I can, I bring her face to mine and part my lips. My kiss is tasting, testing, and it doesn't take long for her to kiss me back. I meant what I said. I don't know what *this* is, but I do know it's something good. I just hope she doesn't expect more from me when I don't even know if I have anything else to give.

I break the kiss and squeeze the back of her neck possessively. "I have to go."

She nods, and we stand up together. "When will I see you again?"

"Soon," I promise, and with one more kiss, this one rougher than the other, I turn to go, wondering why it's so hard this time to leave her behind. "I'll call you and we can go out or something."

"Like a date?" she asks to my retreating back.

"Something like that," I answer back, grinning and actually feeling that emotion inside, an emotion I thought long since dead.

CHAPTER TWELVE
JAGGER VALENTINE

"HOW OFTEN DO you actually do this?" Blake asks me quietly. As soon as the last word leaves his lips, he wraps them around his cup's straw and slurps. There's a bit of disbelief in his tone because he's never staked out the compound with me, and all he knows about my sister is the minimal information that I've ever given him.

I don't like to talk about her. I don't even like to talk about this place because when I do, I remember everything. All the things I try so hard to forget. Like that tree stump just ahead, the one at the beginning of the property...it used to be a whole tree, and at one point it was cut down. A few days later, my father used its surface to cut off a woman's hand for sexually touching a man who was not hers by marriage. My father deemed it appropriate, because even if we could make her clean again, the hand never would be.

The list goes on and on with everything I look at on the property. Each thing has its own horrible memory.

"It doesn't matter," I murmur back. He's been eating nonstop since we got here a little after sundown. Me? I can't stand the thought of food when I'm here. Hunger pains go away, and fear—fear for my sister—replaces them.

"Yeah, it does," he replies. He turns his head to look at the side of my profile. "You're obsessing."

"You would be too if you knew everything."

"So tell me everything then."

I glare at my front windshield, not having the nerve to glare at him myself because I know he's right. He deserves it all, but saying it out loud, sharing it with people, is too painful. It makes it too real when I can sometimes convince myself that it was all a nightmare.

"Give me something, Jag. Tell me what's so scary about living here."

I rake a hand down my face and as I do, I mumble the answer into my palm.

"What?"

With that same hand, I grip the steering wheel tight and grind out, "It's a cult, dude. Nothing great comes from a cult."

"Well, clearly your sister doesn't mind it, otherwise, she would have left by now."

He thinks I'm overexaggerating. This time, I do turn my glare to him. "It's not that simple."

He points at me with his straw. "It was for you."

I slice a hand through the air. "You have no idea what I had to endure to escape and the cost that would have come had I been caught."

He stares at me, observing how my chest is heaving in both fear and adrenaline. My mind takes me back to that horrible night and how it felt to run as fast and as far as I could. It's a memory I can practically touch, taste, and hear.

"How is seeing the therapist going?" he asks so softly that I barely hear him, but it's full of concern.

"Not well." I work to get my breathing under control by rubbing my palms soothingly against the thighs of my jeans. What I would give right now for a shot of whiskey.

What I would sacrifice for a twelve-pack of beer. But I'm trying. I'm working on becoming something that I know Dolly needs. Even if I can't give her everything she deserves, I can give her a sober me. I decided that after I left her this morning.

"Are you letting her help you?" He waves a hand in front of him. "With this bullshit and the shit we endured in the military?"

I give a little shrug and look out at the front of my windshield once more, observing the compound. "Sort of."

"Well, you're not wasted, so something is changing."

I remain silent, and for some odd reason, this is suspicious to him.

"Jag..." he draws out. "What's going on between you and the therapist?"

A spike of dread lights up my nerves because the last thing I want to do is tell him that I have feelings for her. "Nothing."

"Fucking liar. Are you sleeping with her?" The accusation in his tone does nothing for my on-edge mood.

I give a little shrug and, again, refuse to look at him. "It's not what it seems like."

"Sure," he grinds out between his teeth. "You get drunk and you sleep with everyone. How is this any different?"

"Because I went back for seconds," I murmur.

He shuts his mouth, and the silence grows so taut that I finally glance over at my best friend. He doesn't blink for several seconds. "That's..."

"I know."

"You're..."

"I know."

"What does she say about this?"

"She has questions I don't know how to answer."

He blows out a breath. "You've been so out of touch with yourself, even before I met you, that I'm not surprised you don't know how to tell her you feel something for her. Honestly, Jag. I don't know if I've ever seen you sleep with one girl more than once. This is huge."

I suck in a slow breath, and as I exhale, I say, "Part of me feels like I'm using her."

"For what?" he asks incredulously.

I bite the inside of my cheek real hard in hopes that I can keep myself from admitting things I'm not ready for. "To breathe."

"That's not you," he says after a pause. "You don't use people. You're very plain on what they'll get from you, and it's up to them if they believe you or not. I'm sure this woman is no different. She's a therapist. She knows how…"

"Fucked up?"

"Right. I'm not going to call it that. But she knows how damaged you are, and yet she's choosing to continue whatever this is with you."

I think of how I'm going to respond, how I need to come up with something, but all of it shoots out of my mind as soon as I see a thin shadow creep across one of the small driveways, the one that I know leads to the main house—my father's house. Holding our breath, we watch a tall man walk across from one building to the next. I don't recognize him from afar, but that doesn't mean anything.

"I was starting to think no one lived here," Blake whispers.

"Don't let the quietness fool you. At this time of night, they're in prayer."

He snorts quietly. "And how long does that take?"

"It depends on what they're praying over," I mutter disgustedly. I believe in God, but I don't believe in the version of God that they do and the things they think they have to do to win his favor.

When I was a kid, we sat for an hour and prayed together. My father believed in prayer as a group rather than prayer as individuals to ensure that we were being pure and selfless and to make sure we were praying over the things he considered right and just. And if our prayers dipped into what my father considered impure or self-serving...well, I liked squeezing my eyes shut during those punishments. I wasn't, however, shielded from cleaning up the blood.

But it's been two hours, so it makes me believe that something else is going on, something they need extra prayers for. I voice all of this aloud, and he listens quietly without judgment. This is the most I've told him, and it probably shocks him that I'm giving him anything at all.

"I wonder what it is."

"Likely my father."

"What's wrong with your father?"

I wet my lips to keep from smiling. "He's dying."

Blake grunts. "And the world is better for it." He shifts in his seat, and I know whatever he's going to ask next, he's second-guessing if he wants to know the answer. "So what's the plan? How are you going to get her out? And what are you going to do if she doesn't want to leave?"

"Oh, she wants to leave," I whisper with surety. "No one in their right mind would want to raise a baby here, and definitely not with that asshat. And as for what I'm going to do next? I'm going to storm the castle."

"And how are you going to do that?" There's humor in his tone. I don't like it, and all it makes me want to do is punch him in the face. "They don't seem the type to fear having guns. I'd bet they'd light your ass up within minutes of you stepping on their property."

I turn and look at him with one eyebrow raised. "You're going to help me." Before he can protest and say he refuses, I add, "They have outings. I just need to figure out their schedule and the day they'll take my sister along."

This time, he does laugh out loud. "That could take years, Jag."

"She doesn't have years," I say through clenched teeth. "If it comes down to it, if they keep her on the property for the foreseeable future, I will go in there. I will remove her, Blake. I will free her and hide her from them if it's the last thing I do on this planet."

"It very well may be the last thing you do," he agrees. "You're going to get shot."

"Not if you have my back."

He takes his time lowering his cup down to his lap. His expression clears. "I'll always have your back, but that doesn't mean I want to die."

"You had no problem signing up for the military with the possibility of dying."

He frowns. "This is different. We're home."

I point to the compound. "Nothing about that is home. Not for me. Not for my sister. Imagine living somewhere where you constantly fear impurity and pain. That's not home." I shake my head. "That's not safety behind your four walls. That's a living hell."

He breathes deep and then exhales while he thinks for a moment, and then he says, "Fine, but I don't want a murder charge. This isn't our unit, Jag. These aren't orders. This is real shit. This is law. We don't have anyone covering up our crap anymore, so I'd prefer it if it didn't come down to someone's life."

I smirk. "I make no promises."

He rolls his eyes.

CHAPTER THIRTEEN
DOLLY STERLING

AS I STRIDE by the windows of the town's only Asian restaurant, I stop in my tracks. Not only did he text me that he wanted to go out for supper, but he also let me choose the place, and if his body seated at the table inside is anything to go by, he's early.

I expected him to be late, and honestly, I don't know what to make of it.

Perhaps him giving me slivers of the secrets he holds inside was enough to start a change, but I won't remain hopeful. And at this point, I don't think he'd be himself if he didn't somehow let his trauma shape who he is. The trauma is so ingrained that it practically formed his entire personality.

I'm not complaining, I like it. I like him. Okay, so more than like him. But the question that's been running through my head is, does he?

My phone ringing in my dress pocket startles me. I fish it out and observe the blocked number with a frown. The same number tried calling me this morning, but I ignored it because I was in the shower. The only voicemail left behind was just breathing into the phone for several seconds. It was weird, but now isn't the right time to see who is on the other end, so I decline it and go back to observing the man waiting for me.

I smile when he starts tying his straw wrapper into knots and his leg shakes vigorously under the table. He hasn't seen me yet, so I just stand here, soaking in the man who doesn't know someone is observing him.

He truly is strikingly gorgeous. It's sinful how well put together he is. His hood is down today, and I can tell he just got a haircut. The length on the top is trimmed, and the sides are buzzed close to his head. The hair on top is slicked back and styled in a sexy way, and all I want to do is run my fingers through the strands.

The lighting is dim in the restaurant, and the shadow of his edgy jaw plays with the muscles along his neck. And even though his full lips are tight with unease, I still want them all over my body.

The way his foot is bouncing, I can tell he's getting more agitated the longer he waits for me, so I step forward, my heel clacking against the pavement and rustling the leaves.

As soon as I open the door, the fried food and sauces filter into my nose, making my stomach growl, but the food is only the second reason I'm here. I make my way to the first, and once I'm at the table, I tuck my dress under me and take a seat across from him.

"Hey," I say cheerfully, because even though the aroma of the food is powerful, I did not smell a single drop of alcohol when I strode by him, and normally he's heavily perfumed with it.

I see his shoulders relax, and he leans his back against the backrest of the seat. He crosses his arms, almost like he's waiting for an explanation from me.

Frowning at him, I ask, "What? I'm not late." I check my phone as I set it on the table. "Okay, so I'm two minutes late. But technically I wasn't because I was watching you outside of the window for a little bit."

An eyebrow raises. "Stalker?"

"Perhaps," I say, trying to hide my grin.

The table is small enough that he can lean forward. He tucks a stray curl behind my ear without reaching a great length, and his original scent wafts around me like a gentle breeze. "Obsessions can be a dangerous thing, darling. Trust me," he begins, and then his piercing eyes meet mine. Between his confident touch and his intense gaze, my skin heats. "I would know."

I whisper back the first thing that comes to my mind. "I can't help it."

He smirks, and a tiny dimple I hadn't noticed before appears on his cheek. "Did the sheep fall for the wolf?"

"Maybe," I whisper again, blushing so hard that sweat beads down my spine. "Fall" implies that I love him, and I don't know if I'm there yet. Infatuated, yes. Obsessed, yes. Love? I don't know. And maybe, just maybe, I'm preventing myself from going there because I don't know if he can ever return it.

The set of his eyes doesn't harden like I expect them to, like they have each and every time we've talked about my attraction to him, so I'm surprised when there's no warning in his tone as he says, "You should stay far away from me." He slowly takes back his hand and rests it on the table.

"You and I both know that it's too late for that."

"Hmm," he hums, as if he's trying to decide how to talk me out of it, but it's in a way that suggests he doesn't want to.

"If only you would let me in all the way," I murmur so only he and I can hear. The waitress is off to the side, waiting for our moment to be over, but I can tell she's trying to pick up on what we are saying.

He wets his bottom lip. "You know more than anyone else in my life."

"Well, that's a start," I respond, my stomach doing

flip-flops, because even though it's not a lot of information, it still suggests that I'm a trustworthy person, someone he wants to confess things to and someone he definitely has an attraction for, if the way he's watching my mouth is anything to go by. And by the conversation the other day, he has some sort of feelings for me, something that stirs him to keep coming back. But I want to know more. "Tell me something real."

Like the predator he is, his pupils seemingly widen a fraction. "How about when I saw the fear in your eyes in those woods?" His nostrils flare like he's indeed breathing in the scent of my fear. "I can't stop thinking about your body when I caught you. You were so stiff when I took you down, and as soon as I shoved my cock in, your body sang for me. Or how about your tight pussy rippling around my cock the deeper I went, how much you wanted to fear it, and how much it turned you on at the same time?"

My clit tingles, and I cross my legs to apply some pressure there.

"Want to get out of here?" he asks, eyes still on my lips. He must have caught the movement and understood what it meant.

Even though I really want to, I apply a grin and roll my eyes. He seems to use sex to distract, and as enticing as that is… "No. If you can't tell by my figure, I like food."

I wave over the waitress, and she acts like she wasn't listening to a damn thing as she startles into action, brings us the menus, and takes our drink orders. Once she finishes her basic waitress tasks, she disappears back to the kitchen. I pick up the menu, and he opens his mouth to protest, but I cut him off when I see two familiar people entering the restaurant. I hiss, "Shit."

He scowls over the top of my menu before I lift it to

hide my face. It doesn't matter, because within seconds, those same two people are shadowing our table.

"That menu isn't going to hide you, Dolly," Sadie grumbles. She yanks the menu from my tight grip and smooths it flat on the table as if I'd been abusing it.

I cringe as I look between her and Rollo, and then I scowl at how they're dressed. Rollo is wearing a nice button-down shirt and Sadie is wearing a black dress. I don't think I've ever seen her in a dress. "Is this—are you two on a date?"

They glance at each other, and then Sadie turns narrowed eyes at me. "So what if we are? Aren't you?"

"Well...yes." I blink a few times as I come to the realization that I missed every single stolen look between the two of them and made excuses as to why it was occurring. "Shit. I—I didn't know you guys had a thing for each other."

Honestly, I don't care. Rollo and I have been just friends for so long that I don't even remember what it was like to be his lover. And Sadie deserves a nice guy. Who am I to disapprove of such an appropriate match?

"That's because you've been so wrapped up in your own life that you forgot to watch ours," Rollo says, adding a laugh to ease the lashing.

"For shit's sake, Dolly, we came into the coffee shop together. That should have given you a clue that we were together."

I run a hand down my face, probably smearing the makeup I took forever to put on. "Wow," I mutter. "I completely missed that. Well, I mean, sure, I'm fine with it."

Sadie chuckles. "Thanks. We didn't know how to tell you."

"Honestly, I wouldn't either," I begin. "My best friend dating my ex-husband. Sounds complicated."

"But it's us, so it won't be."

She isn't wrong.

"Women," Rollo groans.

As if they just now noticed him, they turn as one, and Sadie greets Jagger in the best way she knows how. "You must be him." And then she frowns. "You look familiar."

Jagger narrows the set of his face as he concentrates on her, soaking in her face. I don't know what he sees, but a clarity takes place, and his expression changes from confusion to recognition.

"Jagger?" I ask so softly that only he hears. That was quite the swift emotional change so evident on his face and the stiffness that returned to his body.

He carefully masks his face and in the deep voice of his, he says, "Sorry, I've never seen you before."

Her eyebrows pinch further together, and she starts scratching at her elbow. I know that sign. It's what she does when she's thinking hard but isn't sure she actually wants the answer.

"You didn't sleep with her or something, right?" Rollo cautiously asks.

Sadie rolls her eyes and slaps him in the chest with the back of her hand. "I don't go around humping every guy. I can count on one hand how many sex partners I've had, thank you very much." She looks back at Jagger, cocks her head to the side, and adds, "I swear to God, I know you. What's your name?"

He flexes his jaw, turns his head toward the window, and refuses to say.

"Jagger, remember?" Rollo says, wrapping an arm around her shoulders.

My attention flicks between the three of them. Rollo looks pleased because he knows Jagger more than Jagger would like. Jagger appears to be pissed that anyone knows his name at all. And Sadie…slowly I watch as her face relaxes and her lips part slightly.

"What?" I ask, expecting her to say where she's met him before. But instead, she folds in on herself. Her shoulders hunch and her fingers clench, and she looks like she'd rather be invisible.

Wrapping her arms around her middle, she murmurs something about finding a table, slides out of Rollo's arm, and disappears to the other side of the restaurant. I don't even see her table by the time she finds one.

"What the hell?" I grumble to Rollo. I grip the table tightly because I just know no one is going to tell me a damn thing.

His eyes are still on Jagger when he grunts, "So she does know you." He turns to me then. "Think she'll tell me? Or even you?"

I blink at Jagger a few times, watching as he observes the outside and tries his damndest to ignore the entire conversation.

"Look," Rollo begins, giving his full attention to Jagger. Slowly, Jagger turns to look at him. I can tell he wants nothing more than to stand, to probably even walk out, but maybe it's because he has respect for me that he doesn't. "I don't know how she knows you, but I do know that you're not someone I'd want my girl or best friend-slash-ex—whatever you call it—around. However Sadie knows you…it can't be good if she runs off to hide, so I'm going to tell you—not ask—to stay away from her."

Jagger glares up at him and finally rises to full height. He towers over Rollo, and I watch on, hoping it doesn't unfold into punches. Both are big, broad men. I don't know how I'd pull them apart. "You have no idea what you're talking about." His voice is so deep that it's almost threatening. Maybe it is.

Rollo doesn't bother glaring back, his tone says it all as he responds, "I'm a cop. I know a thing or two about a bad person when I see one, and you are one of them. I'd tell you to stay away from Dolly, but I know Dolly won't stay away from you. So again, let me tell you, if I see you anywhere near Sadie, I will find a reason to arrest you."

Jagger smirks down at him, and it's enough to tell Rollo that Jagger's not going to give him the time of day, believe his threat, or give one shit about being arrested in the first place. Rollo walks off to join Sadie, shooting me a quick look over his shoulder. He wants me to be cautious, and I am, but I know Jagger won't hurt me. And I know Jagger hasn't hurt Sadie. At least not intentionally. Jagger isn't that kind of guy to go after women with the intent to harm.

Slowly, Jagger sits down, and just as slowly, he lifts his gaze to mine. I cannot read what's behind the mask. Pain, perhaps, but I can't be sure. All I know is, I don't like being in the dark, especially when it involves every single important person in my life.

"What was that about?" I hiss, unable to keep my annoyance from my tone.

His jaw flexes, the muscle rippling over and over again, but he's staying in his seat. He hasn't walked away yet, and he hasn't run to the nearest bar and drowned in a pint of beer. He looks like he wants to, but he's staying, and that's more than I could ask from him when whatever this is is a clear problem.

"Jagger, seriously. Please tell me something."

His hard exterior cracks, and he runs a hand through his hair, messing it up when he tugs on the roots. "I grew up with her."

CHAPTER FOURTEEN
DOLLY STERLING

WE LEFT the restaurant with no food. I could tell he wasn't going to make it through the meal, so I paid for our drinks, and we took off without so much as a goodbye to Rollo and Sadie. Wherever they chose to sit was well out of sight anyway.

With slightly trembling hands, he unlocks his apartment door and pushes it open. It's dark inside, but even before he turns on the lights, I can tell the apartment is a lot cleaner than it used to be. I almost comment on it, but I don't want to spook Jagger any more than he already is.

The lights come on, and my suspicions are confirmed. There are a few beer bottles, almost as if they were forgotten whenever he made a great effort at cleaning his place up. The entire living space no longer smells like beer. In fact, it kind of smells like him. It's a good sign that opening up and having someone to talk to has really helped him in little ways that matter most.

I step into the living room and turn toward him, waiting for him to explain. To say anything about how he knows Sadie. "You have to talk to me, Jag," I begin when he makes a move toward the kitchen for what I hope is a glass of water. He opens the fridge, and my stomach sinks when a bottle of beer appears in his hand. Within a second, he pops the tab.

"Is that really how you want to handle this?" I hiss at him, marching in his direction with every intent on making him see how he doesn't need alcohol to fix this. To fix anything, for that matter.

His hand visibly shakes, and his jaw flexes as he grinds his teeth. He breathes heavily through flared nostrils, and within the next second, he growls loudly and pitches the bottle at the wall. The glass shatters, and beer spills everywhere. I don't care about the act of aggression because whatever is going on clearly is something that's frightening him to his wits' end. What matters is that he is still able to listen and see reason.

I wait for a minute and let him get himself under control. His chest rises and falls, and his shoulders bob with every deep breath he takes. He tightly pinches his eyes closed and stands in his kitchen, ready to bolt or burn down the world, I can't decide which. Am I in a dangerous position? Absolutely. Does Rollo's warning to be careful ring through my head? Yes, it does. Do I give a shit? No, because Jag needs someone, and that someone is going to be me.

I carefully step up to him and lightly grip both of his elbows. His muscles are taut under my touch. "Tell me what's going on," I whisper.

"Run," he whispers so softly that I almost don't catch it.

I frown deeply. "What? No, I'm not going anywhere, Jagger. You can't shove me out."

His eyes fly open, and I take a step back because inside them is so much pain and need, and that predator that lurks below the surface is back in the driver's seat.

A thrill shivers down my spine, and fear makes the hair on my arms stand on end.

"Run, darling." There's such a dangerous edge to it that fight-or-flight kicks in.

It takes me all but a blink to take off back into the living room. I head to one side of the couch, feeling the floor vibrate underneath my feet as he stomps after me. It's a small apartment, and there's no place to run, no place to hide, so I use the couch to block his path to me.

His expression is one of steel, hard-edged and masking everything underneath the surface.

Adrenaline is coursing through my veins, making my heart beat faster and my eyes wide. He stops at the other end of the couch, waiting for me to make a move, waiting for the prey to make a wrong decision. The pressure is high, the anticipation top-notch. I know this couch won't save me for long. All he has to do is take a step and reach for me, and the game is over. He's caught me.

Like a cornered rabbit, I dart to the right, heading toward the hallway. I barely make it past him, his fingers grazing on the cloth of my dress. I race down the short hallway and take a random left at the first door available. It's obviously his bedroom, and just as I turn to slam the door to make it impossible for him to get to me, his arm reaches out, preventing the door from moving an inch.

I hadn't realized he was directly behind me. I hadn't realized that the chase could be over just like that. I stand frozen, unable to move, unsure of where to go to hide, and not entirely sure I actually want to.

The hand that doesn't have the door snatches my neck, and he walks me backward until my spine hits the wall by the foot of his bed. I gasp through tightened windpipes, wiggle around in hopes that I could break free, but his lips land on mine and steal any desire I have left to keep the chase up.

I melt into the hand around my throat, embrace it as it gives me an allowance of air, and I fall deep into the scorching kiss that's powerful with unspoken emotion.

His lips are desperate, hot and heavy, and full of a lifetime of inner pain.

With his other hand, he pushes up my dress, skims the inner part of my thigh with the back of his knuckles, and yanks down my underwear to my knees. They fall off the rest of the way and pool at my feet, where I then kick off my shoes and push them all aside. I want nothing in the way for whatever he has planned. I can be what he needs me to be in this moment. I can be his distraction from all the pain that Sadie's presence brought about.

Repeatedly, his fingers squeeze and loosen around my neck like he can't decide if I should live or die. I know in the end my life will prevail, but it's thrilling to know that at any second, he could decide the opposite, and I won't be able to stop him.

With my underwear gone, he cups my pussy and applies pressure to my clit. I gasp into his mouth, the sound trapped from being choked. He draws circles with the heel of his hand, heightening the sensation and making my nipples harden in an instant. My gasping becomes a strangled moan. He then kicks my feet further apart, and I almost whimper when his hand disappears, but I end up melting against him as a finger slips inside me, instantly rubbing the most sensitive areas within me. I find myself grinding against it to feel more, more, more, until a tiny little spark begins in my lower abdomen. It soon blooms and grows and stretches until it consumes me. My moans turn into groans, and then I scream through the choking as soon as the blazing fire explodes. My pussy clamps around his finger, begging for it to never end.

"That's right, darling," he mutters against my jaw. "Give it all to me."

I ride wave after wave of intense pleasure with every

single nerve in my body lit, exposed, and hypersensitive. I never want it to end, but all too soon it fades, and I begin to whimper, wanting nothing more than to experience it again.

One second, I'm against the wall, and the next, I'm being yanked away from it. He flips me around and pushes my top half against the bed, leaving my ass in the air, exposed just for him.

I hear the quiet zip of his jeans and feel my dress being pushed up my spine, and then the tip of his cock nudges my entrance. It's only a breath before he grabs both hips and shoves inside. I cry out, and if it weren't for his iron grip, I'd have fallen forward on the mattress. He doesn't wait for me to adjust. Instead, he begins to move. His hips are punishing against my ass as he shoves so deep and so hard against me. My groans are low and animalistic, both from a slight pain and force as well as the pleasure of being so full that I almost don't know where I begin and he ends.

The length of his cock rubs every sensitive spot that his fingers had. My breasts tighten against my body, my nipples hardening further into such tight peaks that they ache. His fingers dig achingly into my hips, and I swear it only adds to the pleasure. And the sounds he's making? His own moaning makes me begin to beg him for more.

"Please," I begin, whimpering the word over and over again.

And just like that, he angles himself slightly differently. It hits a whole new unexplored spot, and my entire world lights up around me. An orgasm is ripped from me within seconds, and I scream so loud that my throat goes instantly raw.

My pussy clamps so tightly around him that I hear him curse, and the screams from my raw throat turn into cries of such intense pleasure that tears actually spring to my eyes. It's only when I come down from the high that I hear him speaking.

"Answer me, Dolly," he growls. "How bad do you want to feel that again?"

Like a greedy child, I start to beg once more. "Please. Please, Jagger!"

My entire body is so sensitive, as raw as my throat, that as soon as he reaches around and pinches my clit, using his plowing-into-me motion to rub at the tight nub, the fire instantly begins once more. I can already tell it's going to be just as intense as it was before.

Tears spill over my eyes when he grabs my hair with the other hand and yanks my front half off the bed. The pain from my scalp, the fullness of my pussy, and the pressure of my clit send me over the edge once more. I free-fall into complete oblivion.

My screams echo off his bedroom walls. His pumps become erratic, and I know he's right there with me. His moans and my cries of pleasure mix together in a beautiful harmony, and I'll never forget how the two of them sound together.

My toes curl into my feet, and my fingers grip the sheets as hard as I can stand it. I ride wave after wave, my skin heating to a point where a fine sheen of sweat coats every part of my body. And when I come down from my pleasure at the same time as him, he lets go of my hair, and I slump my top half on the bed, completely spent and totally satisfied. My scalp hurts, my hips ache, the outside of my throat feels bruised, and the inside feels raw.

Slowly, he pulls out, but he quickly replaces his cock with some kind of cloth, apologizing and telling me how he shouldn't have been so rough and asking if I'm on the pill. I distractedly nod because I'm still too far gone, dazed, to answer him with actual words.

When he's done cleaning me up, he tosses the cloth to the side of the room, and then I hear the rustling of clothes, soon followed by the sound of a zipper. Next, he heads to the front of the bed, climbs on, and sits. I watch as he pats for me to rest against his thigh, and it takes all the energy I have to crawl up the bed. Once I reach him, I curl myself around his legs and nestle my cheek on the muscles of his thigh.

I'm so damn comfortable, so damn spent, that I almost don't hear it or care to hear it when he says, "Sadie is the girl that ran away the same night I did."

"The cult?" I whisper hoarsely.

His fingers find my hair, and he starts massaging the scalp he bruised. "Yeah," he breathes out. "The last time I saw her, she'd been pregnant by her father. The very first thing she was going to do with her freedom was get an abortion. I'm guessing she did."

"I'm sorry you had to see her again," I answer after a few seconds. The horrors of their childhood are too much for any child to have to bear, and to know that Sadie had been pregnant by her father? She never told me.

If her life was a nightmare, what was his like? I have every faith that someday he will tell me those things, but right now, I don't need those answers. I can just be here for him, because in the end, that's what he needs most. Not a shrink. He needs my support.

How awful would it be for Jagger and Sadie to reconnect after years of hiding? To each other, they're the living breathing essence of their past. How do you hide from that? You can't.

He doesn't say anything else, and I start to drift in and out of thoughts about Sadie and Jagger, in a sleep I hadn't realized I needed. I don't even care when his phone rings and he jostles me around to dig it out of his pocket.

"Blake?" Jagger whispers into the phone.

I start to drift further, but before I go completely out, I hear Blake say on the other end, "I'll do it. But it has to be tonight or I'll chicken out."

CHAPTER FIFTEEN
JAGGER VALENTINE

THE BREEZE IS BONE COLD, seeping under my skin despite my thick black sweater. My muscles are so damn stiff from it. Hell, maybe I'm not stiff because of the cold. Maybe it's the evil from within the compound I'm standing in, waiting in the shadows with the only other person I trust to have my back.

Either could be true.

The only thing on our bodies that isn't covered in something black is our heads. If I do happen to come across anyone but my sister, I want them to see my face before I put a bullet through their brain. Every single one of them here deserves death. I won't even ask questions. I won't entertain pleas.

We wait in the cover of darkness, checking the quiet grounds. It may be the middle of the night, but there's not a single light on, and there's also not a single person watching the property like there used to be. It makes me question why? People could escape at will. Perhaps there's a reason. Maybe...maybe no one wants to anymore. All those kids who I grew up with that dreamed of escape are probably all brainwashed now into believing that this life is the correct way to live. Knowing all this makes me sick to my stomach, especially when my gaze keeps drifting back to the grassy area by the playground where my father would publicly force me to whip my sister. I wonder if her blood still stains the grass like it had when I ran.

"Now what?" Blake whispers by my side. He checks his gun to make sure that the safety is off.

"Shh," I hush, because that's all I have. I don't know my next move. I hadn't anticipated not running into anyone right away, and for some odd reason, that makes me unsettled. The absence of people changes everything. It makes me suspicious, it makes me feel like tonight might not be a good night.

"Jagger, I didn't want a gun in the first place, but if I'm going to hold one, it's not going to be cowering in the shadows."

I turn narrowed eyes at him. "I'm not cowering, asshole. I'm thinking."

"Then tell me what you're thinking," he grumbles. "I can help you make decisions."

I appreciate that he doesn't point out how my voice is shaking ever so slightly. Adrenaline already screams through my veins, and it's tinged with the acidic burn of fear. I've done things way worse, way more dangerous than this to people more sinister than my father. This shouldn't be any different, but it is. Why? Why is this so different?

The breeze kisses my cheek when I turn back around and glance at all the buildings and houses. "I need to find my sister."

"Okay," he whispers. "Which house is she in?"

"Well." I blow out a breath and point with my gun to the biggest house. "She has a room at my father's, and since he's sick, she's probably taking care of him there."

I make a move forward, but Blake wraps his fingers around my upper arm. "What about the guy she's pregnant by?"

Flexing my jaw once in disgust, I hiss. "It would not surprise me one bit if he took the master bedroom and called it his own."

Blake looks back and forth between my eyes, studying me and my resolve. "You're hoping to run into him tonight, aren't you?" It wasn't really a question but a matter of fact.

"Absolutely," I say so deep that it's sent to the devil himself.

He nods in small little dips of his head and then says, "Well, let's get a move on then." He bumps me with his shoulder, and for some odd reason, his approval gives me what I need to step out of the shadows and head in the direction of the house.

I glance back, watching as Blake melts into the darkness once more. He's only here to have my back, he isn't here to follow me in. We discussed this before we came here, that he would be at my side only when shit hit the fan, if it ever hit the fan. So far it doesn't look like that's going to happen. I go in undetected, and I leave with my sister undetected. It's as simple as that. At least, that's what I'm telling myself.

Tucking my gun into the back of my jeans, I stride with purpose toward the white house. The garden is still maintained, which was my mother's pride and joy that my sister adopted at an early age, so I know she's still here. She has to be. She has enough heart to stand by his side until his last breath, even after all he's done to her.

The house's garden surrounds a wrap-around porch —an all-American house if I ever saw one. I step quietly onto the porch, knowing that one of the boards creaks, and make my way to the front door. I know my father. He keeps all the windows locked up tight, but he always taunted my sister and me by leaving the front door unlocked. It was almost a dare, begging us to try and run just so he could use us as an example whenever someone in the cult started straying. He played mind games like that. As much as he loved watching us afraid of when the whip came out, he loved watching us tremble with just the very idea of it.

Slowly, I reach for the screen door's handle. My fingers tremble all on their own until I firmly grasp it. My nerves are on fire, but I tug anyway. The hinges on the screen door make far less noise than I remember, and I find that just as suspicious as the lack of activity outside. I then grab the knob for the main door and push it open with gentle ease.

My heart hammers in my chest, and I honestly don't know how much more of it I can endure. I shove it out of my mind as best I can, and then I take in my familiar surroundings.

The first thing I notice is the smell. It smells exactly like I remember: laundry detergent and mothballs. To this day, I still cannot use that brand of detergent. Every time I whiff it while out and about, it brings me right back here, back to these memories.

The second thing I notice is how everything is exactly the same. The same furniture, the same position of the furniture. Even the candles are in the same spot. My father's jacket is hung on the same peg by the wall. His spit-shined shoes are in the same spot by the door, and the keys to his personal van are on the end table by the couch.

Everything is the same, yet oh so different. Instead of standing here as a caged boy, I'm a free man. Maybe not to my demons, but essentially, I'm free. I use that to calm my racing heart and my fast thoughts.

With one foot in front of the other, I head through the spotless living room and stand before the dark stairs. I know that he lives on the second floor, the same as Issy and me when we were kids. My bet is that if she isn't in the master bedroom with Tyron, she'll have the same bedroom as she had before too.

One step at a time, I push my way up the stairs and into the dark abyss of the second floor. It takes until I'm at the top for my eyes to adjust. The scent of the laundry detergent is stronger up here and I try like hell to not cover my nose.

Being so close to my father, knowing he's in this house, on this floor, does nothing to calm me. The hair on my arms is standing on end, and every sense I have is heightened no matter how many times I tell myself that everything will be fine.

I creep toward my sister's room, the first room on the left. Mine is to the right, and my father's is down the hall. I don't dare look into my room. What if it's the same? Like I never left? I don't think I could handle it if it still looked like I still lived here, so I avoid it entirely.

My sister's door is cracked open, so with a quick look around me, I gently push it further. My eyes are wild and wide, fear making my muscles shake and ache at the same time because…it's empty. Her room is entirely empty. There's no bed, no dresser, no rug. The only thing that remains as it once was is her pink curtains from when she was a baby. I remember my mother having picked those out while she was pregnant and my father hating them when she brought them home.

I stand there like a fool, dumbfounded that I chose wrong. She isn't here, and that leaves only one place left: the master bedroom. But then…which room is my father's? I slowly spin in a circle as my mind spins with questions of uncertainty. How am I supposed to get her out if I don't know where she is and he isn't?

"She isn't here," a familiar voice croaks.

My spine straightens, and the nerves on the back of my neck prickle. *Fuck.*

"Come out of there, Jagger," my father continues, and then he starts coughing. "I know it's you, and you won't be able to hide from me."

I briefly close my eyes, knowing he's right. I'll never get out of this house without facing him. Slowly, I turn to leave Issy's room, take the gun out of my jeans, and step back into the hallway with it at my side.

With more bravery than I thought I could muster, I swivel to face my father in the dark, and I find that I'm not the only one holding a gun. "You look like shit," I comment, because what else am I supposed to say to the bastard besides the basic truth? He does look like shit. He weighs a whole lot less than he did when I was a child. I can see his collarbones on his too-big shirt, his cheekbones are more prominent, and his eyes look sunken in. Even from here, in the shadows, I can see the dark circles underneath them. Hell, he barely looks like he has enough strength to stand for much longer.

"Is that any way to greet your father?" He may look sickly, but his tone is just the same as it always has been: cruel and final.

I decide not to answer him. Instead, I raise my gun from my side and point it at him. "Where is she?"

His eyebrows raise, and for a second, I see myself in him because I have that same look. It's enough to place my finger on the trigger because all I want to do is obliterate anything that makes me resemble him. "She hasn't lived here since she got pregnant."

"Fitting that even she would let you die alone."

He chuckles, but it sends him into a coughing fit. "I'm not worried about dying alone, Jagger. I'm pure, I have God, and God has me. I'm never alone."

"You're delusional if you think God will let you anywhere near him."

He smiles but cocks his head to the side. "Why are you here? Why now, son?"

The word "son" feels like a punch to the gut, and I snarl in his direction. "To save Issy."

"You'll never get to her. Besides, I'm not entirely sure she'd go with you willingly. She's quite taken to the Temple after you left. Seen your errors and learned from them."

I point my gun at him as if it were an extension of my fingers. "You told her I was dead. What else was she supposed to do?" Plus, I know that as soon as I give her a taste of freedom, she'll know exactly what kind of life she should want and will have. I just need to get to her first.

He shrugs. "It was the only way to get her to stop waiting for you to come back for her and to embrace the life she was meant to have here."

I narrow my eyes on him. "What did you tell her? About how I died? What bullshit did you feed her?"

There's no emotion on his face when he says, "That I found you in the streets and shot you in the back of the head."

I take a threatening step forward, and he raises his gun to meet mine. "You're a fucking bastard." My voice is animalistic, as monstrous as the demon I feel inside, rising its ugly head after being beaten down for days on end.

With his free hand, he holds up a finger, and I note that it takes everything he has to just lift his arm. "God will look past my lie because it steered her toward the truth. You, on the other hand"—he raises his gun ever so slightly with an arm almost too weak to hold it—"will go to hell."

I open my mouth to respond, to tell him I'll meet him

there, but his gun fires and I fall to my back. The pain is what I feel next, white-hot agony in my gut. I don't even realize the breath had been stolen from me until I try to take the next one.

A shot to the stomach. I've had worse, I've felt worse, but I have no way of knowing if the bullet hit something vital. I need to get up, though. I need to face him, to put an end to this before my own end.

It takes everything I have to get off my back. Surprisingly, the gun didn't fall from my hand when I was knocked off my feet. So, I gather myself into a sitting position even with every single nerve lit with agony and point my gun at him…and then I stop.

He's smiling at me, but this time the gun isn't poised at me. It's poised at his own head.

He begins murmuring a prayer, one we say to those who are dying in our group, and in the next instant, before he's even finished with the prayer, the gun goes off.

Blood sprays the bedroom door behind him before his body crumbles.

The gunshot rings in my ears, and for a second, my world stops spinning.

Numbness takes over my emotions. I've seen people die a hundred times. I've seen people's brains being blown out, half of them my fault, but this one…this one is different. He was my greatest enemy and to watch the life leave his eyes…

Relief should fill me. It doesn't. Satisfaction should overcome me. It doesn't. Instead, I'm consumed by this numb feeling, watching blood seep from his head wound out onto the floor. And for a second…

For a second, I mourn who he should have been.

I sit there for several heartbeats, one hand holding my wound and the other hand still gripping the gun. I know

I'm getting weaker, I know I have to move, and I know I have to get out of here and get to a hospital before I end up in hell with him.

Dolly's face appears in my mind, and it's enough to find the energy to peel myself off the floor. It isn't easy, and it doesn't happen without screams of pain, but eventually, I make it somewhat to my feet. I stumble toward the steps and carefully climb down each one. Once I reach the bottom, I grip the wall to steady my waning balance. Blood smears on the wall before I wobble to the living room. I just need to get to Blake and get the fuck out of here.

I don't know how I got there so quickly, but I yank open the front door, and just as I fall to my knees on the front porch, Blake's arms swoop under mine.

"He's dead," I tell him as he helps me to my feet. He throws my arm over his shoulders, and he immediately starts getting us off the property at as quick of a pace as I can manage.

"And you will be too if we don't leave right now."

CHAPTER SIXTEEN
DOLLY STERLING

"HEY," someone says. Their tone is desperate, and it takes a while for their voice to register through my sleepy mind. A shake to my shoulder comes next, and I groan my displeasure at being woken at what surely is the middle of the night.

And then it hits me…I don't know that voice.

I crack an eyelid and nearly scream when I see a man bending in front of Jagger's bed, his hand on my shoulder as he tries to jostle me awake.

Instead of screaming, I gasp, grab the blankets, and tighten them around me as I scoot away from him. He stands up to full height, and his facial features get lost in the darkness of the room. I can see his outline when he scrubs at his hair, though, he has to be as tall as Jagger.

"Shit. Um…" He pauses and takes a step back. "Don't freak out."

"Who the hell are you?" I look around me in the dark and try like hell to make out anything in the shadows. I can't. "Where the hell is Jagger?"

"He's in the living room, but—"

"Get the hell out," I growl. I feel threatened, and I certainly didn't approve of having Jagger add his friend into the mix. That is not my thing.

He holds his palms out to face me. "Whoa, calm down. I'm not—no. Look, I—we need your help."

I scowl when I hear nothing but sincerity in his tone because I sure as shit can't see it on his face. "With what?"

"Jagger's hurt. I don't know what to do. Stitching people back up was never my thing. It was another guy's on the unit, and he doesn't live in Oregon anymore. I—"

I slice a hand through the air to get his rambling to stop. Clearly he's in a lot of stress. "What are you talking about? What do you mean Jagger is hurt?"

"Get off the bed and follow me," he says. It wasn't in a rude way, but instead, it was desperation for me to believe him.

He heads around the bed and exits out into the dark hallway. As soon as he enters the living room, a lamp is lit and a moan quickly follows. "Hold on, man, she's coming," this man says.

My heart skips a beat, because everything he said—the fact that Jagger is hurt—comes rushing to my mind as facts and truth. I scramble out of the covers, and as soon as my feet hit the floor, I'm dashing out of the room. What I find in the living room is something I wasn't necessarily ready for.

Jagger is slumped back on his couch with a white towel pressed to his stomach. The towel is soaked with a crimson color. It takes me a minute, but I realize that that color is blood. Real blood. I've never seen so much blood in my life.

I stop in my tracks and swallow thickly. His face is ghost white, and sweat drips over his cheekbones, disappearing after his jaw. I expect his eyes to be wild, but they're not. They latch onto mine with a calmness that any normal person wouldn't have. But Jagger isn't normal, and this probably isn't unusual for him, if some of the stories he has warned me about are even a sliver of the truth.

"Wha—" I begin, unable to find the words. I can smell the scent of his blood filling the room, and it makes my stomach churn for just a second. Now that I can see him more clearly, I look at his friend. He's far more stressed out than Jagger is, tugging on the roots of his hair with bloody hands as he looks back and forth between me and Jagger. "Did you stab him?"

His eyes fly open wide. He places a hand over his heart and says, "I would never!"

"Then who stabbed him?" I demand.

"I was shot," Jagger corrects. He moans as he readjusts the way he's sitting and then turns his gaze back up at me. "And Blake didn't do it."

I sit there and simply blink at him. Two minutes ago I was falling asleep on his leg, and now I've been woken by a stranger—Blake—to find Jagger lounging on the damn couch with a damn bullet in his body! My hand flies to my mouth to wipe at it as I try to comprehend everything that I don't know yet.

"Say something, darling," he purrs at me.

My eyes narrow, and I take two angry steps in his direction with my finger jabbing at him. "I went to sleep, and you were fine. I wake up, and you're shot. Not only are you shot, but you don't seem to care that you're bleeding away into a damn towel! Don't you dare 'darling' me!"

"I'm not going to die," he says coolly. I swear to God, if he had a cigarette in his free hand, it would be picture perfect. He may be saying all that, but does he hear the weakness in his own voice? Does he know he looks like he's knocking on death's door?

"What the fuck happened?" I ask, directing my attention specifically at Blake, because I know anything

I ask Jagger means it will take forever to get straight answers.

Blake pinches the bridge of his nose and sits on the edge of the couch's arm. "He went to get his sister."

"He went back to the cult?" My tone holds no waver, even though a sliver of fear curls in my gut for whatever he had to endure there.

Blake drops his hand. "Yes. I heard the gunshot, then another, and I ran to the house and caught this guy before he collapsed on the porch. His father is dead, by the way."

I turn wide eyes to Jagger. "You killed your father?" I hiss.

He rolls his eyes and then his neck. "No. He killed himself, but not before he shot me."

I curse under my breath and lower myself to my knees before him. Slowly, I peel the towel away to see the wound. Blood seeps out of it, slowly but surely. I do not, however, see the bullet at all. It's buried deep. I cringe a little as I press the towel back down because he can't hide his pain. It's in the way he tries not to moan and in the way his stomach muscles recoil at the slightest pressure I apply. "And your sister?"

He catches my gaze, and I watch as his face hardens. "She wasn't there."

My frown matches Blake's. "Where was she?"

Blake is the one who answers, and I'm glad for it, because I don't think Jagger could answer me anyway with the amount of anger radiating off of him. "We couldn't find her. I didn't see her outside when I was watching his back, and she wasn't inside where she should have been. We don't know where she is."

"I do," Jagger growls. "She's living with Tyron. She's living with her new pedophile husband, and I'd bet every dollar I own that this was all his idea."

Standing once more, I place my hands on my hips and try to remain calm. What he did tonight was very, very stupid, and from what Sadie has told me about the cult, he's lucky he's alive at all. "Can't she just leave now that your father is dead? Can't they all?"

Jagger's jaw flexes. "My father said something about everyone being highly devoted now. Tyron will replace him, and it'll be like there never was a problem with power."

"This is so fucked up," Blake murmurs. "You should have left immediately when your sister wasn't there, man. You entertained your crazy old man and got yourself shot."

"Yeah, well, at least he's gone," Jagger sighs out. "Are one of you going to take out the bullet?"

"Hell no," Blake says at the same time I blurt, "Absolutely not."

His eyebrows raise into his pale forehead. "You want me to get it out myself?"

I sneer down at him. "If you don't knock it off, I'll murder you myself. You're going to the hospital whether you like it or not. I assume you came here because you both thought I could?" They both nod. "I hate to tell you that just because I have 'doctor' before my name, it doesn't mean I know how to yank a bullet from a body. You're going to the hospital, or I'm dragging your body to the morgue. Take your pick."

My breathing is heavy, and he watches me with interest. I'm so mad I could spit fire. And then he has the audacity to smirk. "Scared, darling?"

"Stop! No 'darling.'" I slash a hand through the air. "Yes, okay! Yes! Is that what you want to hear? You're bleeding out on your couch, and all you're doing is smiling!" I then give Blake's shoulder a little shove. "Pick him up. We're taking him there whether he likes it or not."

Blake bends to do just that, and Jagger all but growls at him. "I can fucking walk," he says so deep that it sounds like an angry bear.

Both Blake and I step back, and I want nothing more than to give him another piece of my mind, but that can wait for the car ride. Right now we need to focus on getting him back in the car so I can make sure he lives to breathe for tomorrow. He has to. He may seem fine, but he isn't. This is Jagger, surviving in unsurvivable conditions. But one of these times his luck is going to run out, and over my dead body will it be in front of me. Over my dead body will it be while we're together, or whatever we are.

The very thought of his death springs tears to my eyes, and I try like hell not to let the panic win.

It takes all the effort he has, but eventually he gathers himself to his feet on his own. Blake makes a move to help support his weight, but Jagger slaps his hand away and starts walking toward the door.

"This is so stupid. You are being so stupid!" I say as I stride after him. "You're going to at least let me help you down the stairs."

Blake gets ahead of Jagger and opens the door, and without waiting for an answer from Jagger, I pull his arm over my shoulder and tug some of his weight onto myself. Thankfully, he allows it without any complaint. I can, however, feel his labored breathing against my ribs, and my fear spikes just a little more.

"I am so mad at you right now," I hiss under my breath.

Blake takes the first step down, and I line Jagger up for the same. But Jagger doesn't move. He doesn't scoot an inch closer. I look up at him curiously, and just as I do, he collapses on his apartment landing and takes me down with him.

CHAPTER SEVENTEEN
JAGGER VALENTINE

A STEADY ELECTRONIC beeping is what brings me back from my deep sleep. The sound of footsteps and voices quickly follows. I squeeze my eyes shut because all of these sounds beat against a headache, reminding me that something is wrong with my body. It brings me right back to the gunshot sound, and I flinch as though it's happened again. My abdomen aches and burns at the same time, and I open an eyeball to see what's been done to me.

The first thing I see is the hospital room that I'm in, the walls made of baby blue curtains. I've never been in the recovery area in the States before, but I imagine that that is where I currently am. I curl my fist and then lift my hand, checking out the IV needles sticking out of my skin.

I hear a voice grow closer outside my curtain and follow it along until it reaches the opening, where it's then whipped back, revealing the man. Even with the phone up to his ear, I recognize Rollo immediately, even in his police uniform. He looks me up and down and then sighs, stepping into my makeshift room and closing the curtain behind him while ending the call with whoever he had on the phone.

"I'm glad I was given your case before anyone else,"

he grumbles. "You have no idea the shit story you've likely caused."

"Where's Dolly?" I ask as I attempt to sit up straighter.

Rollo comes forward and lifts a remote from my bedside, adjusting the bed for me to a better seated position. I don't bother telling him my thanks because he looks like he'd rather punch me than receive my gratitude.

"I had her wait in the waiting room. No one is allowed to see you yet, since you just got out of surgery."

Surgery makes sense. The bullet must have been deeper than I thought. "Then why are you in here?" I close my eyes against the headache that now owns a heartbeat.

"The badge gets you a lot of places, and my captain sent me here for a gunshot wound victim," he says distractedly. "Have you seen the wound yet?"

I shake my head, still with my eyes closed. "Do I need to?"

In a matter-of-fact tone, he responds, "You should see the mess you've caused, yes."

This time I do look at him, but through narrowed slits as my anger begins to rise. Who the fuck does he think he is? He doesn't know me, he has no idea what's going on. "I don't fucking know you, and you don't fucking know me. Let's leave it at that."

I want to tell him to fuck off, but since he's wearing the uniform and likely here officially, I better bite my tongue on certain things I want to spew in his direction. Like how he's overstepping because he knows me through someone he cares about.

He grabs onto the rail of my bed and tries to seem threatening as he leans into it. To everyone else, he might appear that way, but to me, he's just another dude who needs to mind his business.

"Put yourself in my shoes, Jagger. If your ex-wife, someone you consider your best friend, calls you in the middle of the night and tells you that her boyfriend collapsed from a gunshot wound, and then you had to call an ambulance for her because she couldn't form coherent sentences, how would you react? Not to mention getting your ass quickly to the station to get assigned the case to protect her."

I flare my nostrils, chiefly because, again, it's not his business, and second, because I don't like that Dolly was scared for me.

"That's right," Rollo whispers, studying my face. "She loves you. She was afraid you were dying, and let's face it, you were. You may not have a fear for your own life, but she does, and if you died in her arms, she would never recover from it."

She loves me. That rings in my ears over and over again, co-existing with the headache. "You have no idea how she feels about me," I mutter deeply, but he catches it anyway.

"Oh, I do. I know her well, and I know you're more than just a project to her now."

I breathe deep and then blow it out through my nose, unsure how much of that I want to process right now.

"What happened?" Rollo asks after a few minutes of silence.

I look away from him, not wanting to completely incriminate myself. Even though I did nothing wrong, I still broke into my father's house. I still trespassed onto his property.

"Dolly already told me what you'd told her. Are you really from the Savage Temple?"

"Yes," I admit reluctantly. "I didn't kill my father. Don't pin that shit on me."

"The Temple hasn't called in any death, so I have nothing to investigate there. Not yet, anyway."

I frown at him. "You're going to ignore what I said? Why?"

He raises his eyebrows at me and then crosses his arms. "I may not be in love with Dolly, but I still love Dolly, and if you're what she wants, I can't stop her. I can only help her, and pretending I didn't hear what you said is the best thing for her. Just get your shit together, man. Be a man for her."

I don't know why, but I admit something that I've been holding on to for a while now. "I don't know if I can be any better than what I am."

He grips my shoulder. "I think she knows that, but it'd be helpful if you didn't go around getting shot."

I give a little shrug, and it's enough to get his hand off my shoulder. "I need to get my sister out."

"She's an adult," Rollo begins. "She can leave whenever she wants."

"You have no idea what you're talking about," I growl.

He clucks his tongue a few times as the room grows taut and uncomfortable. "I do know the Temple has a lot of outside people in their back pockets. Important people. Even people at the station. Are you saying that she wouldn't be able to leave if she wanted to?"

"That's exactly what I'm saying, and for those very reasons, she can't even run away."

"Hmm," he hums, but just like me, he doesn't know what to do about it either. He's bound by the law, whereas I'm bound by trying not to kill them all. "I recognize the look on your face, and I'm not going to advise you not to do anything, but if it comes down to it, I may not be able to turn a blind eye."

"Is that a threat?" I ask, raising an eyebrow at him.

He shakes his head, and I do not like the sympathetic look on his face when he speaks. "Just trying to look out for you. If you do something so stupid and so public, I won't be able to help you. Right now, we—you, me, Dolly, and your friend—have this under wraps. I don't know how long it's going to stay that way, but I'm hoping forever. I'd appreciate it if you could figure out your sister situation before shit hits the fan, but if not, there'll be nothing left for me to do but arrest you."

I don't have time to respond as the doctor comes in and Rollo steps aside for him. Dolly quickly follows with Blake hot on her heels. In my peripheral vision, I watch the doctor's mouth moves as he updates me on my condition, but I don't pay attention. The only thing I'm looking at is Dolly's face, how tired she looks, and how that's my fault. Being shot may not have been a big deal for me, but it is for her. It just makes me question if I really want to keep her by my side, not for anything she can't give me but for what I can't give her.

The doctor leaves, and I didn't hear a word he said. Dolly and I continue to stare at one another until eventually, Blake and Rollo disappear. Only then does Dolly approach my bedside.

"I could kill you," she breathes out. She lifts the blanket, then my gown, and looks at the gauze surrounding my incision. For a split second, she closes her eyes.

I take her hand, knowing she needs some part of me and hoping that I'm able to give that to her. At least for a second before I do what I have to do. "I know," I mutter. "I'm not..." I pause, scowling down at our joined hands as I try to come up with the right words. "You know that I'm not good with relationships, neither friendships nor lovers. Blake was the only person in my life until you came along. I don't know how to have them, and I think..."

"Don't," she whispers as tears gather in her eyes.

"I'm too dangerous for you."

"No, you're not," she immediately says.

"I was shot, Dolly."

"That was a freak thing." Her tone is pleading, but there's an edge of anger to it. She knows where this is going, and she doesn't want to accept it as the right thing to do.

"It'll likely happen again in one form or another, and we both know it. Unless Savage Temple disappears, I'm too dangerous for you. Aside from that, you deserve what I'll never be able to give you." *A real man,* I want to add, but I don't.

My gut twists by what I'm doing, but I know that in this moment, I'm doing the most unselfish thing I can think of.

"You do deserve this," she hisses through incoming tears. "You deserve me! Please, Jagger. Please don't let this night color us wrong. We can find a way around the Temple. We can finally get your sister out, and then we can disappear. Please, Jagger."

With my free hand, I scrub at my face and work past the lump forming in my throat. "If you sat back and looked at the whole picture, you'd know it won't work that way, and you'd know I'm right."

"So what?" She lets go of my hands and crosses her arms over her middle protectively. The tears fall freely down her cheeks. "This is how you want things to end? This is how you want me to walk away from you because I'll suddenly realize that I don't love you?"

The word "love" is a slap to the face, and I wince. All it makes me do is feel worse because she's not the only one who has deeper feelings than attraction. But if I focus on that, I'll never let her go. I inhale long and slow to work past these emotions I haven't felt since I was young. "We need some time apart. We need to clear our heads." *And you need to see that I'm no good for you.*

"Jagger, please," she whispers. The words are finished with a tiny hiccup.

I swallow thickly. "Leave, darling. Let me give you what you need. Please, leave. And don't look back."

She breathes deep and long, her eyes pinched tightly shut. Instead of leaving right away, she rushes forward, and her lips immediately find mine. The kiss lingers with everything she doesn't know how to say and everything that I feel and can't say. I taste her tears, I taste her pain, but I know she'll have far more tears and far more pain with me than without me.

And then she backs away, turns on her heel, and strides out of my makeshift room.

And somehow, this feels more like my death than the gunshot wound.

Blake whips back the curtain with a frown on his face. "What the hell happened?"

I look down at my palms, the cracks and crevices of my skin lined with my blood. I know…I know this isn't the end. Not with the Temple. Not with freeing my sister. And not with my life hanging on the line. I know that if I go on that property again, I likely won't walk back off. She doesn't deserve that, and she doesn't deserve my shortcomings as the partner she needs. As a man, I am no good for her, and I cannot give her what she's meant to have.

"I'm saving her."

CHAPTER EIGHTEEN
DOLLY STERLING

TEARS STREAM down my salty and raw cheeks as I walk up Rollo's driveway, heading directly for his house, where I know Sadie will be.

When I left the hospital, I had kept it together long enough for Rollo to stop me in the hall and tell me where I could find Sadie. He knew what had happened, he heard it from outside the curtain where he'd been waiting with Blake. With the compassion he usually shares, he gave me a hug and told me he'd see me at his house after a bit.

I need them both right now—my best friends, my ride or dies. This hurts far more than my other breakups. I had really started to see a future with Jagger, I had started to think we could be more than just a couple. I thought he'd eventually open up to me further and we'd have something that could last a lifetime. He has to know that I never expected him to ever be the dream guy, I love him just the way he is. Why can't he see that we are worth it, that we should fight for it? That even though he will never be fully capable of being an ordinary guy, we could be extraordinary together?

I know his self-worth is low. It's a problem with him, and somehow, I have to get him to see that he's worthy of feeling love, having love, and experiencing love.

In the light of an autumn sunrise, Rollo's house is a bright yellow color. It's normally pale yellow. He picked the siding himself a few years ago, despite Sadie's and my protests about going with something a bit more modern. He didn't listen, though.

There are a few low-maintenance plants dotted here and there, but since it's fall, their leaves are wilting and brown. He keeps his lawn perfectly trimmed, something that both Sadie and I tease him for, because he has to be better than his neighbors and have the best lawn on the block. It has to be a man thing, but he will never admit that the competition drives him to mow twice a week whether it needs it or not.

Folding my arms around my middle, I trudge up to his house through the leaves that drifted over from the neighbor's yard in yesterday's wind. I don't bother knocking. Instead, I angrily wipe my tears with the back of my sleeve, grasp the handle, and step into the familiar living room.

This isn't the house that Rollo and I shared together. We lived in an apartment for the majority of our marriage, especially while we were both going to school. We certainly didn't have the dog that comes barreling at me, even though I kind of wish we did.

I bend to one knee right away so that Captain, Rollo's golden retriever, doesn't tackle me. He's too large for his own good with not enough brains, but it makes him even more lovable. He skids across the living room's hardwood floor and comes to an abrupt stop before me, punctuating the official greeting with a sloppy kiss to my nose. I wipe it away and then scratch his head, giving a few kisses myself.

"Hey boy," I manage to croak out. "Sadie here?"

Having heard my entrance, because Captain's paws were thunderous when he ran toward me, Sadie's head pops around the corner from where the kitchen is on the other side of the wall. A concerned look immediately takes over her face as she notes the tear stains on mine.

With grapes in hand, she strides into the living room and directly toward me. "Did he die?" she asks quietly, taking a seat on the couch and patting the cushion for me to do the same. She pops a grape in her mouth and offers me one.

I shake my head, both at the food offer and her question. "No, but he would have. The doctor said he wouldn't have survived much longer had he not gotten to the hospital when he did."

Sadie curses as she chews on the grape. "Did you eat breakfast?"

I shake my head again, and she hands me another grape. This time I take it because I know she won't stop until I get something in my stomach. "Are you tattooing today?" I ask. "Am I keeping you from your clients?"

"I canceled my day when I heard…when I heard about Jagger."

I can tell she's frustrated that he went back and even more frustrated that he managed to get shot. Her emotions and thoughts are out there in the open for me to read. Even though their connection was a long time ago, that place will always bind them together in one form or another, even if they now have no other connections that are beyond it. She cares whether he lives or dies, and she clearly doesn't approve of the way he almost died.

"What about you? What about your clients?"

Slipping a hand through my tangled hair, I blow out a long breath that's quickly followed with a hiccup of leftover emotion. "I took the morning off." I look down at my hands and start tracing my fingernails. "How well do you know Jagger, Sadie?"

I haven't talked to her about him and how she knows

him yet. Jagger just told me last night, and even then, he didn't give me much to go on.

"Is that what you really want to start with? Or do you want to talk about how he broke your heart?" It must be obvious that he did, since I'm not by his side.

I glance at her, but only for a split second because the concerned expression is too much for me right now. "I don't want to talk about that yet."

"Okay," she whispers, blowing out a breath. "Honestly, I've blocked out a lot from my past, but I can try to give you answers. What do you want to know?"

Shrugging a little, I lean back into the couch, letting the thick cushion swallow me up. "Anything."

She pauses for a good long while, and during that time, I refuse to look in her direction. Instead, I settle in for any tidbit of information I can glean off of Jagger and why he makes the choices he makes. Maybe then I can have peace while I figure out how I can endure the coming weeks without him, perhaps the coming years, if it comes down to it.

"Savage Temple is on a compound, and on that compound, I lived close to the leader's house—Jagger's house. I suppose you could call us neighbors, even though there was a good amount of space separating my house from theirs." She clears her throat as emotion clogs there. "It was far enough away that Jagger said he could never hear me scream when my…when my father would come into my room. He told me that if he had, he would have come to help me."

That sounds exactly like Jagger, and I bet it only made him angry that he never could tell when she was getting abused. "Were you close?"

I can hear her shrug when her clothes rustle. "Yeah, as close as two kids could get in such a hostile environment.

He knew what was happening in my house, and I knew what was happening in his."

"And that was?"

Again, Sadie clears her throat uncomfortably. "I was getting raped in mine, and he was getting beaten in his."

A tear quickly gathers in my eye and streams down my cheek. My heart hurts for the both of them. I cannot imagine what that was like, especially while I had such a normal and loving childhood. Maybe this is where the problem is, maybe this is the disconnect. I don't know where he's coming from because I've never walked an inch in his shoes. He's trying to save me from having to. But I don't need saving.

She continues, "By all rights, he was a good kid who loved his sister. His father just found excuses to do what he wanted to him, to make an example out of him. Jagger's punishments were public, mine were private. Even so, we sort of bonded over it, as best we could anyway. One night we made a pact to run away and planned the whole thing. When that day came, we bolted and never looked back."

I look at her now, watching as her eyes carry a faraway look while she dips into the memory she probably wishes she'd blocked by now. She continues, "I thought he was dead."

"Why?"

She meets my gaze. "We may have run in the opposite direction just in case one of us was caught, but I never thought I'd never see him again. I thought we'd connect, find a way back to each other, and find a way to survive together. But that never happened. Instead, I found you." A small, sad smile appears on her face.

I grab her hand and squeeze, then I hiccup as emotion takes over once more. The grief for what I'm losing is small in comparison to everything they lost as a child, everything they were supposed to have and didn't receive: love. "I think running from things is so engrained in him, and it started that day. It built up over the years of his childhood, and when he saw freedom from the hard life, he took it." But he didn't really become free, did he? He went into the military, where he endured the punishing instead of the punishment.

"Do you think that's what he's doing now?" she asks softly.

"Maybe," I answer honestly. "I think he doesn't know how to have what he wants, and I think he thinks he isn't good enough for it anyway."

She squeezes my hand back. "Do you think he also doesn't want to hurt you because of who he's become?"

I snort. "He's an idiot if he thinks the person he is is going to hurt me."

"It is kind of romantic though, if you think about it, coming from someone like him."

My brows pinch together. "What do you mean?"

"It's obvious," she says, chuffing at the end.

"What is?" My frown deepens as I get further and further confused.

"He loves you as much as you love him. The only difference is, he doesn't know what love is. He's never experienced it, except for his sister, and even then, that's moved past love to obligation. To survival and then the guilt for leaving her behind."

"Yeah," I whisper, knowing she's telling the full truth.

My phone begins to ring. I dig it out of my pocket and sigh deeply.

She leans over to glance at the screen and the numbers displayed across it. "Who is it?"

"I don't know. They called me at the hospital but I didn't answer, and that's not the first time they've called." Obviously I was busy and in no place or mood to answer a call at the hospital. I had let it go to voicemail, but no voicemail was left in the end.

"Answer it now," she mutters, leaning back and resting her arm against the back of the couch.

I shrug, clear away my tears, and answer the phone. "This is Dolly."

There's a rustling on the other end, and the female voice that comes through is quiet and mousy. "Hi, um... are you the therapist?"

I turn a scowl at Sadie. "Yes, yes, I am. Can I help you?"

The woman's voice is just above a whisper, and I get the feeling that she doesn't want anyone around her to overhear. Not uncommon with those who suffer from domestic abuse. "Can I schedule an appointment?"

"I'm sorry," I answer with as much sympathy as I can muster at the moment. "I am not taking any new clients. Maybe try back in a few months?"

The woman on the other end sighs and then immediately hangs up. I pull the phone away from my ear and do a bit of sighing of my own before dropping it in my lap. "Yet another person I cannot help."

Sadie leans forward and gives me a side hug. It's unusual for her because she doesn't like touch. I lean my head on top of hers and take in the comfort she's trying to give, knowing that in the end, I at least have someone.

Rollo's front door opens, bringing in a chilly morning draft, and he steps inside while greeting a happy dog. He doesn't say a word as he sits across from us in a recliner and steeples his fingers in front of his face while Captain sits in front of him and begs for attention. "Do I have to give advice?" he eventually asks.

I shake my head. "I just need time to think."

"You do know that the Savage Temple are dangerous

people, right? They'll come after him and anyone he's with. Jagger's friend is in danger, and so are you." He points his steepled fingers at me. "I'm keeping Sadie here for protection, and I'd like to do the same for you."

I try hard not to roll my eyes. "I don't need protection."

He pinches the bridge of his nose. "You do. You don't know who you're dealing with. They have the means to make a body disappear, Dolly. Why do you think they haven't called in their leader's death? They have acres and acres of private property to bury a body so deep, we'd never find it."

"Nothing is going to happen to me," I respond, even though my voice wavers because now I'm not so sure. What if he's right? What if I am actually in danger?

"For all we know, they could have been watching Jagger for a while. They could know he's in town. They certainly know that someone was in that house with Jagger's dad because Jagger left his own blood behind. They could have taken that blood to the police station and had it evaluated without anyone else knowing but the people they pay to be on their side. Or they could have looked into the gunshot victim that was brought into the hospital. Both would be easy to do. His secret is out, Dolly, whether you like it or not, and it wouldn't be hard to connect the two of you."

I let go of Sadie and throw my hands up in the air. "What do you want me to do, Rollo? Hide? I won't do it." I won't prove Jagger right. Even if I can't physically be by his side, I can still metaphorically stand by his side.

Rollo's nostrils flare, but he knows he can't force me to do what I don't want to do. He sits there for a moment, trying to wrestle with his anger, and then he abruptly stands, disappears down the hall to his bedroom, and comes back out a few seconds later. When he's standing before me, he passes me a small gun. "Take it, and keep it with you at all times."

"I'm not carrying a gun."

"You are. When you leave your house, you take it with you."

"Why are you doing this?" I demand softly. "Why are you making me do this?"

He bends to one knee and gets eye level with me, still holding out the gun for me to take. Even though my words say I'm not going to, I still take the gun from him. "Because Sadie and I both love you, and the last thing I want to do is show up at your crime scene, if there ever is one to find."

I stare at the gun for a while, weigh it in my hands, until I finally realize how right he is. "Okay," I whisper.

"Okay?" he echoes.

I nod, and he leans forward and pecks me on the forehead.

"Okay," he adds one last time.

CHAPTER NINETEEN
JAGGER VALENTINE

I SURVEY THE FAMILIAR BAR, the one I haven't been to since the night I met Dolly. I try like hell not to meet Blake's gaze because it has a permanent disapproving edge to it, but he forgets that he's here with me. He has a beer in his hand just like I do.

It's been two weeks since I was shot, and while I probably shouldn't be drinking, it's all I've been thinking about. It was a matter of time before I gave in, just like it was a matter of time before I had to give up Dolly.

I haven't called her, and she hasn't called me. What would I say? Anything I want to say would just end up with us back together, and I still firmly believe that she could do better than me, that I'm not what someone like her deserves. And maybe...since she hasn't called me or showed up at my apartment, maybe she finally understands what I'm talking about.

But why does all that make me so livid? Why does that drive me to drink? All she's doing is exactly what I want her to do, and yet, I have fire in my veins. It only gets worse when I imagine her being fucked by someone else, leaning into someone else, looking at them with her doe-eyed sparkling gaze of affection.

"One more beer and then we are leaving," Blake mutters to me over the music.

I grunt my approval, even though I have no plans on obeying him tonight. What the hell is he going to do? Drag a full-grown man outside and force him into a car? I highly doubt it. He will likely just leave me here with his buddy's number. His buddy owns a driving business. And then he'd then check on me in the morning before slapping me around a bit for all my stupid choices. Let's be real; I know this choice is beyond stupid, but I need one night—just one—where I don't think about her. Where I don't want to hunt her down like every instinct in me is demanding I do.

It wouldn't be fair for her or for me. It's not what she deserves, and it's not what I deserve. What I deserve is this beer and to spend an eternity alone.

How can one girl get me so wrapped up in my own bullshit? And after such a short period of time? It doesn't make sense.

"I can see your brain whirling," Blake adds. "Talk to me about something, Jag. Anything. Give me something about what led you here tonight."

I bow my head and shake it slowly. "You don't get it."

He takes a swig of beer, letting me collect myself because those few words were held with such raw emotion. "Then make me understand. Dolly is just a woman. You've had plenty."

I look at him now. "When you're me, you search for a way to forget." I hold up my beer in emphasis. "Just seeing her made me forget. Something like that isn't easy to lose and it sure as hell isn't easy to let go of."

"Because you're punishing yourself." His chuff is annoying as hell. He leans back a little and crosses his arms over his chest.

"What the hell makes you think that?"

He shrugs as if it's obvious. "You think you're a monster, and monsters don't deserve good things."

"Fuck off," I grumble. I lift the bottle to my lips and take three big gulps just to ease the sting of his words. "Even if I am, it still doesn't change the fact that she deserves more than what I am."

This time, he snorts. "Why don't you leave that up to her? Let her figure out what she wants and what she thinks she deserves. All anyone deserves is proper love. It doesn't matter what kind of package it comes in." He leans into the table conspiratorially and whispers, "I hate to tell you, man, but you love her, and she definitely loves you."

I look away as if I'd been slapped. "You don't know what you're talking about."

"Sure I do. I know you. I know you better than anyone, even more than a therapist would, you know, if you saw one who you didn't end up having feelings for. I know all your dark and dirty secrets. I know what makes you you. And I know that whatever happened to make you the machine that the government took advantage of left you incapable of knowing what love actually is."

I glance down at my bottle of beer, flexing my jaw while watching the droplets ring around the base of it. It's always infuriated me when he's the voice of reason. He was on our missions, and he has always been since we've been home. My mind doesn't want to accept his answer, it doesn't want to turn it into advice, but my heart is willing to entertain what he's saying anyway. The two have been at war with each other since the moment Dolly left the hospital.

My emotions are so damn raw, so damn potent, that I'm surprised I haven't combusted.

The door to the bar opens, and I frown as Rollo strides in with another cop. "Shit," I whisper when he heads straight for me. They're both in uniform, and his partner has his hand on the hilt of his gun. I don't move an inch, even though my body is telling me to run. Whatever they want is obviously not something good.

Blake turns around just as Rollo approaches our table. "What's going on?" Blake asks him.

"Jagger, I'm sorry," Rollo breathes out.

"For what?" I ask, eyeing him and his partner suspiciously.

"I have to take you in for questioning."

I hang my head, knowing that this was eventually going to happen but hoping it never would. "My father?"

"Yes. Someone called in when they overheard you at the hospital." I note that he doesn't mention that it was him that the person overheard me talking to, but I suspect that if Rollo gives himself away like that, we're both in deep shit. "And since you were both there, I'm arresting you both."

"On what grounds?" Blake growls.

Rollo doesn't look at him. He keeps his eyes on me as he says, "Right now, just trespassing. We will be in contact with Savage Temple about the death that was reported by an anonymous caller."

For fuck's sake. I put down my beer, and together, Blake and I stand up. There's no point in fighting, so I obey while grinding my teeth. Thankfully, Rollo and his partner let us walk out without cuffs.

As soon as we get to the police station, we're sat down in chairs next to the interrogation room. Ashland isn't large, and therefore it doesn't have a large station. It's not like movies where everything in the station is cliquey. Ashland's is more of an open floor plan business office, minus the cubicles, than anything else.

As soon as Blake sits, he puts his hands on his face

and scrubs at the skin. It's going to be a long-ass night and maybe even the next few days. We might have a chance of proving our innocence with my father's death, but we cannot prove that we were not on the property. There are many ways that could help prove otherwise. It's just a matter of how many charges Savage Temple wants to press, and beyond that, what they're going to do with me when they find out I'm still alive, that I was there within their reach.

If they haven't already.

Right now, more than ever, I'm happy I let Dolly go because I don't know where I'm going to end up after this, and I'd definitely take her down with me.

I slump back in my seat and take in what's around me. It's late at night, so there aren't many cops or others here. A janitor mops the front entrance, and a woman still in uniform is asleep, her head resting on her desk. Rollo and his partner are at the other side of the small office, standing by a set of windows and talking in hushed tones. I can tell the partner is mad, and Rollo is trying to calm him down. The hand gestures tell the whole story. Now, more than ever, I wish that the constant gunfire of my past didn't deafen my hearing.

"My clients are not going to like this," Blake grumbles into his palms before he drops them to his thighs. "I'll be lucky if I have any by the time we leave here."

At this moment, I make a mental note to protect Blake at all costs. I'll get him out of this so that the Savage Temple doesn't take him down too, especially to get to me. "I won't let anything happen to you," I whisper to him.

"What are you talking about?" he whispers back.

"Just keep your mouth shut and let me talk. Don't say anything, and don't go against a damn thing I say."

"I'm just as guilty as you are for going on the property."

I peek at him before returning my attention to Rollo and his partner. "That's not the way I'm going to spin this, and you're going to let me."

"Why?" he asks after a pause.

Still watching the cops, I breathe deep and blow it out. "Because it's time I stop dragging everyone down with me. My problems are my problems. They should never be yours too."

"You're an idiot." His voice comes out as a hiss. "Don't you think people want to help you? Don't you think they care enough about you to want to be that person for you?"

"You're not going to be that person here, Blake. You're going to let me take the fall for this. Please," I beg, for probably the first time since I asked my father if I could stop whipping my sister. "Do this for me."

I finally look over at him and watch his jaw flex with irritation, but he says nothing else, so I take that as a good sign, a wordless agreement that he plans to listen to me. I focus my attention back on the cops, but I do a double take because they're no longer alone.

"Who is that?" Blake whispers.

There, standing with Rollo and his partner, is a woman wearing a conservative dark blue dress that goes down to her ankles. But even though all I'm seeing is her side profile, I know exactly who it is.

"My sister," I whisper back.

We watch with rapt interest, and all I want to do is know why she's here. How she got here. How she left the property without anyone knowing. Or maybe they do know. Maybe they're all outside.

I do a quick look out the windows that face the

parking lot and only find one van. To my surprise, no one else is in it.

"What the hell is going on?" Blake eventually asks.

"I have no idea."

As discreetly as she can, an envelope is exchanged from my sister to Rollo's partner, and I have no doubt in my mind that that's an exchange of money. His partner tucks it into his inside jacket pocket, and I watch as Rollo hangs his head and faces the other way with his hands on his hips. Whatever is happening, he's not fond of it. He's obviously being bought out to cover something. *Fucking Savage Temple.* And to be so out in the open about it.

My sister doesn't even look at me before she turns and hustles out of the station. My heart aches a little at that, but I try to see it from her side. She can't be caught showing much emotion toward her brother, not so out in the open like this, not where it can get back to the wrong people. That doesn't stop me from wanting to shout after her. I want to know what's going on and ask her to stay here where she's protected, but she and I would be fools for thinking anyone is protected from the Temple here.

Watching out the window, I see her get into the driver's side of the van and pull out of the parking lot, taking a piece of my heart with her because I know she's headed back to the cult with no other choice. When I turn back around, Rollo is before us, and he looks far more exhausted than he did a little bit ago.

"Your sister has set the record straight," Rollo grumbles.

"You sound like that's a bad thing," Blake grumbles right back.

"It is when it's paid off." Rollo looks pointedly at me. "I don't want you arrested any more than anyone else, but I also don't want the Temple to have a say in who gets arrested and who doesn't. That's not how I want my city to be run. Now, I've never met your sister until tonight, but I'd love to know why she's here and not Tyron."

"Tyron usually does the business with you guys?"

He nods. "Always. She's taking a giant risk by being here if you ask me, because there's no way they'd let a woman handle their business." He sighs deeply. "Just do me a favor and don't do anything stupid. Don't do anything that will make me arrest you again. Now"—he pauses and makes a big sweeping gesture with his arm toward the front door—"you're free to leave."

I nod, and he starts moving away, and as soon as he's far enough, I turn to Blake. "We're going back tonight."

"What?" he says, completely confused.

"We're getting her out of there before they realize she has left at all." At all costs, even my own life, I will get her out of there, and my own life could very well be the actual cost. "Head home, grab your shit."

I tell him where I'll meet him, and he scowls and asks as I stand, "Where the hell are you going first?"

"I have something I have to do," I say as I stride away from him and toward the station doors. I don't want to go to hell with regrets.

CHAPTER TWENTY
DOLLY STERLING

POUNDING on my front door rattles all of the pictures on my dark hallway's walls. Angry and annoyed, I stomp my way to the offending sound. It's late, and I had just fallen asleep, and now someone is on my front step practically breaking down my door.

In the living room, I whip back my curtain to get a good look at who would do such a thing, fully prepared to call the cops if it's some drunk having lost his way or one of my clients is having some sort of crisis. Either way, I shouldn't have to deal with it at this hour.

I squint into the darkness, then reach over and flick on the outdoor light when I see a familiar silhouette. I double blink.

Jagger is standing in the drizzle, his hoodie pulled over his head, soaked from the elements. He lifts his hand to knock again because he hasn't seen me in the window yet, but he definitely knows I'm up now since I turned on the light.

One side of me is ecstatic that he's here, that he's even thinking about me enough to make the trip to my house. The other side of me is dreading whatever he wants because my chest still aches when I think about him and how he broke it off…how he practically abandoned me like all the others have done to me.

I've had two weeks to think about it, and every day of those two weeks it's festered.

Letting go of the curtain, I wrap my robe tighter around me for comfort and unlock the door against my better judgment. I really am not ready to face him, but if I were one of my clients, I would advise them to step before their fears and work through them instead of avoiding them. It's time I start taking some of the advice that I so easily dish out to others.

Besides, we live in the same town. I cannot avoid Jagger forever.

Holding my breath in order to keep my emotions in check, I grab the handle and swing open the door. Our eyes lock, and the wild and panicked look in his eyes eases to familiarity. To comfort, even.

I want to throw my arms around him. I want to cry on his shoulder and beg him to take me back, to reassure him that whatever he thinks he is, I can handle. That whatever comes our way with the cult, I can endure. I'd do anything for him. But instead, I say, "What do you need?" more softly than I intended.

Raindrops drip down the bridge of his nose and along his jawline as he murmurs deeply, "You."

My eyebrows rise. "What could you possibly need from me? You made it clear that you didn't need me at all."

"That was a mistake that I'll never forgive myself for." He lowers his hood despite the weather so that I can see the honesty on his face. "I have a lot that I'll never forgive myself for, but this one..."

His voice trails off, and he hangs his head in shame. I don't offer for him to come in out of the rain. I don't ask all the questions rattling in my brain. Instead, I just feel my heart pounding behind my ribs because he's saying all the things I want him to say. He's confessing, but...

"What is it that you want from me, Jagger? I can't be an object you just throw away and pick back up whenever you want."

He flinches at my harsh tone, but I'm not going to hold back from him. I never have, and I'm not going to start today.

"I was trying to protect you." He lifts his gaze once more and looks me square in the eye before roaming my face. His study of me is almost as if he's checking to see if I'm still the same woman he knew a few weeks ago. I haven't changed, but it would seem that maybe his mind has.

"I don't need protection," I answer honestly.

"I know," he murmurs.

Even though he's lowering his voice, I raise mine. "I don't think you realize how often I'm in danger with my job, and not once have I not been able to handle myself!"

"I know."

"Rollo makes sure of that, and the schooling and training for my job, all under great minds, has made sure of that!"

"I know," he says in all but a whisper.

My volume rises two notches. "My name may be Dolly, but I'm not a fragile doll, Jagger! And you can't hide yourself from me because you think I should be with someone else! I'm not—"

He stops my rant by taking a step into my house. My mouth snaps shut when he invades my space, grabs my chin, and kisses me. I cannot help it; all the fear in the world about losing him and all the anxiety about having him back collide until they completely melt each other away with his touch. His lips slide against mine, and I respond exactly the same, devouring his mouth, his scent, and everything that makes him him.

"I will always want to protect what's mine," he whispers.

He tips my chin and angles my mouth for a deeper reach to punctuate what he declared and everything he hasn't yet. His tongue slides against mine, teasing and tasting. I shiver when he inhales me deeply, and I nearly moan at the rumble that sounds at the back of his throat.

Gently, which is unusual for him, he pulls away, my chin still in his hand. All the fight is gone from me until I open my eyes and look back into his. As he searches my face, memorizing the lines and dips and slopes, his expression becomes primal and animalistic, and I know exactly what that means.

My heart skips a beat once, then pounds really hard twice.

I step out of his embrace and warn, "Jagger."

He wets his bottom lip, visually sweeping me from head to toe. I can tell by the set of his lips that he knows I'm wearing nothing underneath this robe. "Darling?" his deep voice rumbles. "Did you know I dreamed about your pussy every fucking night? And I'd wake up and have to take a cold shower just to stop my cock from being painfully hard? And yet here you stand…"

"Jagger," I warn again.

"Fucking gorgeous," he purrs. "All fucking mine, too. Or are you going to deny it, darling? Are you going to tell me it's too late for me to apologize?"

"No, but—wait. Wait," I begin as he advances, forcing me to back up into my living room. "We have to talk, we can't just—"

"I've never been good at talking," mutters the monster inside. "I'm best at showing, and if you're telling me that you're still mine…"

"You can't just hunt me down whenever you want to!" I shout at him half-heartedly. My adrenaline starts to spike because the way he's looking at me is like I'm a snack. It makes me afraid and aroused all at the same time.

"Run, Dolly," he warns. My back bumps into the couch, and I quickly scoot to the side. "I've spent my whole damn life trying not to drown in the bullshit I'd been handed. But I can chase, capture, and fuck the only woman who will breathe for me when I can't." His smirk turns wicked when my back hits the wall by the kitchen entrance. "Run, darling. Fucking run."

And I do. I take off into the kitchen and slide around the corner of my island. His strides are much longer and faster than mine. One second his feet are on the ground, and the next he's hopping on the island and sliding across the surface on his hip with fluid ease.

I squeal and dash around it once more. My heart hammers into my ribs as I make a run down the hallway, hoping to get into my bedroom and somehow hide from him in there. But I don't make it halfway down the hall before a strong arm wraps around my middle and tugs me against a solid body. With all the movement, my robe's tie starts to unravel, and Jagger's growling and triumphant chuckle tickles my ear.

The shiver that crosses my body has nothing to do with the temperature difference when he parts my robe, palms my breast, and slides his hand all the way down to the juncture of my thighs. A quick but rough nudge to the inside of my feet with his wet boot has them moving further apart. Deliciously, he skims my sensitive clit. A breathy sigh escapes my mouth and my head drops back onto his damp shoulder as I let him touch me however he pleases. His fingers are wet and slick from outside, a cold touch that only arouses me further.

"Even if I ask you to walk away, you can't escape me," he whispers in my ear. Gently, he angles my head in one direction with his cheekbone, and then he latches on with his teeth to the crook of my neck. The pain is immediate, but he soothes the skin with a lick and wordlessly apologizes by reaching further down my sex and inserting a finger in one smooth motion.

I shiver again as his cold finger slides in and out of me, and his warm mouth covers my chilling skin. His finger starts fucking me faster, harder, and my knees begin to shake as they hold up my quivering body to both the assault of his mouth and the wicked ways of his finger. Little moans whisper past my lips, and they just grow hotter and heavier as the telling curl of heat surfaces in my lower gut. Every time he inserts his finger, the heel of his palm applies pressure to my clit, and his teeth tease the sensitive flesh along my neck. All three are an assault I wasn't prepared for tonight, and I shut my eyes tight to it, just trying to survive what I hadn't expected but had wanted so desperately.

"You'll never outrun me, darling. Even if you tried, you'd never get far," he mutters deeply against my skin, fucking me faster and faster with his fingers. Any other time, with anyone else, I have to concentrate to orgasm. My sole focus can only be what's happening to me, but the way that Jagger approaches sex and pleasure is entirely different than anyone else. He yanks it out of me, gives me no option, and this time is no different. I scream as the orgasm rocks my entire body. His arm around my waist is the only thing keeping me on two feet.

I rock against his finger, against his palm, and ride out the wave while he teases my flesh. And when I'm done and breathing hard, he doesn't give me a moment's rest. He turns us as one and pushes my front against the wall. The hand around my waist takes both of my wrists and pins them against the wall above my head. His rough fingers chafe the skin, but it only adds to my arousal.

The next thing I hear is his jeans unzipping.

"Do you know how much I want you, Dolly?" he asks, his voice like quiet thunder. "Do you know how much I need you?"

Anticipation builds in my chest because finally, I'm reconnecting. Finally, he's here, and he's touching me. He's saying everything I want to hear and everything that I need to hear. And then the skirt of my robe is shoved aside, and my ass is quickly guided backward. He shoves his cock inside me, and I moan and nearly melt against the wall. He fills me up so damn deep that all I can feel is him. His hard stomach is against my back, his strong arm has caged mine, and his thick thighs are firm against the back of mine. All I can smell is him. All I can hear is him. He is everywhere and everything, and all it does is make me feel so damn wanted.

"Fuck," he moans, resting his head against my spine and allowing a moment of stillness, of just feeling one another.

His fingers tighten around my wrists as he starts moving. I can't wiggle an inch. With his hand barricading mine and his other hand holding my hips firmly in place, I'm outmatched. Even if I wanted to run now, I couldn't. Even if I wanted to reposition myself, I couldn't. He has me cemented exactly where he wants me, and there is no escape from everything that is Jagger: his words, his body, his soul. He hands them all to me as he starts pumping in and out, murmuring promises and praise.

My moans stretch through the hall, and a fine sweat breaks out on my back. I can feel his damp clothes slide against my bare thighs and ass and feel the bite of his zipper against both cheeks. All it does is add to the sensations.

The slapping of his hips against mine mingles with the sounds that are coming out of both of our mouths.

His voice becomes deeper and deeper the longer we join as one, the closer I get to orgasming, and the tighter I tug around his length. The impending orgasm makes my skin heat impossibly hot.

"Fucking come for me, Dolly," he demands through gritted teeth. "Do it. Claim me."

My body listens to his demand, and I explode around him, throwing my head back and screaming to the ceiling. He pounds and pounds into me, cursing in such a deep voice that I don't truly understand the words.

In the next moment, he's pulling out of me, flipping me around, and pushing me to my knees. He's pumping his cock, his eyes half-hooded and his lips parted in anticipation, before he guides my mouth to the tip of him and shoves it between my teeth. I taste myself as he rocks into me, but my sole focus remains on his face even as he blurs when my eyes begin to water.

Moments later he's coming, his neck straining and his jaw clenching, the muscles rippling over and over again as he pumps every last drop into my mouth. When he has nothing left to give, he lets go of my head. The look he gives me, the utter adoration drifting my way from him, warms me. He won't say it, I know he won't because I don't think he even knows how, but it's then and there that I realize that he really does love me. That maybe my friends were right.

He lifts me to my feet and softly places his lips on mine. "I'm sorry."

"For what?" I whisper, even though I know what he's saying.

"For all of it. For asking you to walk away, for leaving you to yourself for days, and then for fucking you for my own selfish needs."

"I needed it as much as you did."

He rests his head against mine. "Forgive me?"

I nod as I breathe him in, and not one ounce of me thinks I'll regret ever forgiving him. Maybe I let him off easy, but in the end, I know he did it for unselfish reasons. I know that, and I also know that he's aware of the mistake. I open my mouth to voice just that, and my phone starts ringing from my bedroom. He looks in that direction, and his wet eyebrows crease together.

"Expecting someone to call?" he asks.

"No, not this late." I leave his embrace and head down the rest of the hall. Once I enter my bedroom, I reach and grab my phone from the nightstand charger.

I immediately groan when I see the number and declare, "I'm not answering it."

"Why?" he asks from my doorway.

"It's just the same person calling me over and over again."

His head cocks a little to the side, and he crosses his arms over his chest. "Who?"

I weigh the phone in my hand like it's a brick pulling me down. "Some woman. I never get the chance to ask her name. She calls at least once a day and asks if I have an opening yet."

"What do you tell her?" he presses. The concern is laced in every word.

I give a little shrug. "I tell her no, and then she immediately hangs up before I can say anything else."

He waits for a moment, thinks it all over, before he voices, "I don't like that."

The phone stops ringing, and I set it down. "It gives me bad vibes too."

"Maybe you should block the number," he says, and it's more of a strong suggestion than a piece of advice.

I nibble the inside of my lip. "Maybe. Maybe she's just desperate. I'm sure it'll be fine." I breathe deep and turn to him, a faint smile on my face. "Spend the night with me?"

He shakes his head, and my heart drops to my toes. "I'm going to get her out, Dolly."

It takes me a moment to understand what he's talking about, but it finally clicks. My lips thin in disapproval. "Your sister?" I know he feels obligated to get her out, but I don't like that he risks himself for it. He escaped. She's an adult and could figure out how to escape. There are dozens of hotlines for this purpose. The fact that she hasn't just pisses me off because all it's doing is putting Jagger's life in danger.

He nods. "She's bought herself trouble, and if I don't get her out tonight, I don't think there will be another night."

I hug my middle tightly, a bad feeling swirling in the pit of my gut. He leans forward, cups both sides of my jaw, and presses a soft kiss to my lips. "I'll find you as soon as I get her out."

CHAPTER TWENTY-ONE
JAGGER VALENTINE

"WE ARE NOT GOING to your father's house this time," Blake says loud and clear over the howl of the wind. His hair pushes every which way, and my sweat-shirt clings to my body as the gale embraces me. I don't know why the wind suddenly picked up, but I'm grateful for it. It'll cover any and all noise that we make.

"Agreed," I growl out as I push forward, cutting through the breeze that's shoving me back out the way we came.

We had pulled right into the compound when we arrived, straight onto the gravel drive. We didn't bother parking somewhere discreet. By now they know I'm alive, and by now, they know I've come here for my sister once, and I'll come for her again. But I bet they didn't think it'd be back so soon. After all, I'm still recovering. Every determined step I take, I get a twinge of pain that radiates to all of my limbs. I ignore it because while they may now know about me being alive, they also have to know that my sister has already played a part in the grand scheme of things.

She's more important than my pain.

Every time I think about it, my heart flutters. They'll come for her head whenever they feel like striking, just like they'll do mine if I'm caught tonight. However, I have no plans of being captured in any shape or form. We have a plan of our own and the same guns as last time to back us up. This time I won't be asking questions first. This time I'm shooting first, especially that bastard that got my sister pregnant.

"You got the handcuffs?" I ask him.

He pulls them out of his coat pocket and jingles them in my peripheral vision as we march toward what I know to be Tyron's home. On his way out of the station, Blake stole them off an officer's desk.

He pockets them again so that he can hold his gun more correctly. "I'd still like to know why she didn't stay at the station once she had us released. Why didn't she ask for help from us then? Why did she come back here?"

"Because it's what she knows," I explain, hoping I'm right. "Once you're here for so long, you don't know anything else. You get brainwashed into believing that these are your people, your home, and where you'll belong until the day you die." I saw it happen as a kid, watching the adults be curious about a normal, outside life but never taking that step to escape what they've always known. I wasn't about to be that person, and I won't let my sister endure it any longer.

As we approach the house, I note that not a single light is on. Not that I thought there would be. It's the middle of the night, and the entire compound is dark.

Still, it baffles me that they have no one watching the grounds tonight. Do they think so little of my capabilities? Perhaps they do. They don't know what I'd become after I left here. They don't know how I'm not afraid to kill, how I can sneak into someone's house without them ever knowing until a bullet is in their brain.

But I'm not going to do that to Tyron. Sometimes I

think killing is too quick. Too painless. Instead, I'm going to make him suffer—for Sadie, for my sister, and for everyone else he couldn't keep his hands off of. He will live the rest of his life in utter pain, and that's a far greater deal for his victims than a swift end.

Tyron doesn't have a porch like my father does. It's just a plain house with steps up to the front door and an unkempt rock garden surrounded by broken and half-buried red bricks. A curtainless bay window is off to the left, while smaller bedroom windows are to the right. I can see my sister's touch in the flowers that have long since died with the cold, their pots squatting in certain thought-out places to make the small "property" look more feminine.

"What's the plan?" he asks when I step up to the front door and find it locked. I knew it wasn't going to be that easy, but I had hoped I wouldn't have to break in. That takes time, time we may not have if the wind decides not to be on our side anymore.

I don't hesitate. I stride to the rock garden, pick out one of the only sturdy bricks, and chuck it at the bay window. Blake covers his head as glass flies everywhere, but I don't bother, even as I feel the nicks against my exposed cheeks.

Let me bleed. Let them know I came back.

I march forward with another brick in my hand and break the rest of the glass so we can get inside without slicing up our bodies. Once that's done, all we do is hop, and we're in.

As soon as my feet are on the living room's beige carpet, I immediately hear cursing from within the house. The living room is plain with a wooden rocking chair, a green couch from the eighties, and there is no TV in sight. There's a brand-new computer between the open living room and the cluttered dining room, and I'd bet everything I own that it's used for less than ideal things. Kiddie porn, contacting his pedophile buddies. He'd otherwise have no reason to have one, if he doesn't even own a TV.

What does my sister do when he brings home a child of the Temple? Does she pretend it doesn't happen? Is she around when it happens? What could she really do in the end anyway?

Rage fuels me as stomping sounds down the house's hallway. Naked, Tyron rounds the corner with an old and battered bat in his hand, and Blake and I immediately raise our guns. He stops in his tracks, and my sister, who had followed him, bumps into his back before tightening her robe around herself. At least she had the bright idea to cover herself up, but it makes me sick to my stomach that they were in bed together in such an intimate way. The imagery disgusts me, so much so that I envision driving this gun into Tyron's mouth and firing at will just to erase it from the back of my skull.

A sneer overcomes Tyron, mostly hidden behind a bushy red beard he decided to grow since the last time I saw him at the grocery store. His voice is thick, full of sleep's rasp. "I knew you'd come back. Everyone else thought you wouldn't bother when they saw your blood on your father's floor. Thought you'd be too scared to, but I knew better."

Blake laughs out loud, a rare moment when normally he's quiet during situations like these. "You have no idea," he murmurs, but Tyron doesn't spare him a glance, as if he were completely invisible.

"Tyron," I greet over the top of my aimed gun.

"Did you come for your sister?" he taunts further. All of his jiggly bits shake when he laughs loudly, but I let my brief silence answer for me. "She's my property now, boy. And that's my baby in her. You're not taking her anywhere."

I decide to let that lie because we both know I'm walking out of here with my sister whether he likes it or not. I have the gun, he doesn't. "Are you really that lost without my father that you didn't know to post a guard when the Temple is threatened?"

He narrows his eyes at me and tightens his grip on the bat. "So damn disobedient, so damn mouthy. I could have sworn your father beat that out of you."

I hear my sister inhale sharply at the mention of our childhood abuse. It makes me wonder if she endured anything at all when I left, or if she lived in the quiet hell of obeying.

I smirk. "He tried."

He nods at the gun in my hand, again ignoring Blake and Blake's weapon. "What are you going to do with that gun, big boy? You going to shoot an unarmed man?"

"Yes," I say clearly, and then fire the gun at his foot without a second of hesitation, and damn does it feel good. His howl can probably be heard on the moon.

Issy scrambles out of the hallway when Tyron drops the bat and cradles his foot while balancing on the other. At the same time, Blake and I rush forward as both of us slide our guns into our waistbands as we do so. We grab him by the underarms and drag his ass to the rocking chair. It takes a bit, but we yank back his arms behind the chair, and Blake fastens his wrists to the spokes with the handcuffs. They make a satisfying click, one I can hear above Tyron's screams.

Blake and I, heaving from the effort, step back. "Dude, shut him up," Blake hisses, covering his ears.

I rear forward and punch Tyron in the nose, getting a sick satisfaction out of the crunch that follows. The screams stop, and moans replace them as blood gushes from both his nostrils and his foot now.

"Thank God," Blake whispers in relief and uncovers his ears.

"You're a bastard," Tyron groans out.

I bend to a knee before him, ignoring the fact that my pants are kneeling in a puddle of blood. "I get to be a bastard, Tyron. Do you know why?" He turns his attention fully to me instead of the pain he's in. "For all the children you raped, for the justice of them. And what about my sister? Hmm?" I can see his eyes roll, not from attitude, but perhaps he may be passing out soon. I grab his chin and force him to look at me. "Did you rape my sister too? Did you force her to be with you?"

"I don't have to tell you jack shit," he slurs. A blackout is a very real thing at this point, and if I'm going to give in to my deepest fantasies here, I have to do it fast.

His avoidance of the question is all I need to hear. I look back at my sister quickly, noting that she's silently crying next to Blake while holding her stomach—with their child—and then turn back to Tyron. Rage has replaced the blood in my veins, because even though I'm getting my sister out of here, that baby will always remind her of him once it's born.

I'm going to make this bastard pay for everything he's done.

Next to the rocking chair is a ball of yarn and two knitting needles. I pick the needle up and weigh it in my hand. From the looks of it, it appears to be bamboo, but it's wide at the top and skinny at the point.

I grin as I hold the needles up for him to see. His eyes are rolling again, so I slap his cheek a few times. "This will do, don't you think, Tyron?"

It takes a minute, but he focuses on what I'm holding.

There's a moment of confusion, then fear as I glance down at his dick.

"I'm not that same boy who ran from this place. I'm not that scared teen, that frightened child. I couldn't care less about my future, but my sister's? My father may have done some damage, but you fucked with it the most."

I grab his dick and put the tip of the needle near the urethra. His breathing becomes hitched, knowing for sure that the amount of pain coming is probably more than he can endure. I continue, "I'm a monster, Tyron. A machine that simply destroys. And I'm going to destroy any chance you'll ever have again at having any sort of sex life."

And then I shove the needle in and feel it puncture something near his groin. He screams at the top of his lungs as I rise to my feet, watching blood pour from his nose, his foot, and now his dick.

My sister is sobbing openly now, and by rights, I should kill him, but I'm not going to. I'm just going to make his life a living hell. I take the gun out of my waistband, bring it to his balls, and listen to Tyron plead for only a few seconds before I pull the trigger. The second set of screams are just as loud as the first, until they die out once he passes out.

I take in a deep breath, smelling the copper tang of blood, and then turn to my sister. Her fear radiates off of her in waves, and I pray to God it's fear of the man we're leaving behind for someone else to find. I take two big strides to reach her, and then I grab her cheeks and force her to look at me instead of the blood and the mutilation of Tyron's appendage.

"It's over," I whisper to her, hoping to ease the wildness of her eyes. "It's over. We can leave now."

"You have no idea what you've done," she whispers

back. For a second, I worry that I don't, but then I remember that this is her world and she knows nothing different. She'll thank me once she settles in with me, once she realizes she's free and safe.

"Come on," I say, grabbing her cold hand. "Let's get out of here."

CHAPTER TWENTY-TWO
DOLLY STERLING

JAGGER'S SISTER, Issy, sits in front of me. The couch's massive cushions seemingly swallow her whole, and even more so with Jagger practically glued to her side. His arm is around her shoulders to give her some sort of comfort. I can clearly see she's not accepting of his attempts. In fact, I think it's having the exact opposite effect.

The two of them arrived fifteen minutes ago, just as the sun was coming up. When I opened my front door, Jagger's first words to me were that he didn't know how to get her to stop crying. Of course, I invited them inside. I don't know what he wants me to do, but I suppose I'm better at figuring out what's going on in her brain than Jagger is. I guess I was just more surprised to see that he got her out and that he was unharmed after I found out the blood on his clothes wasn't his. I quit asking questions after that, not wanting to know the details.

I watch as she looks at my socked feet. When they got here, I immediately got dressed and made her a mug of tea, which is sitting in her lap, completely untouched. It's not even steaming anymore. But sometimes it's the act of hospitality or the act of holding the tea and its warmth that can calm someone down. It did work a little, but by her soundless tears falling down her cheeks and her distant look as she studies my feet, I know she isn't necessarily with us right now.

Finally, I break the silence. "What all did you do that made her this way?"

Jagger spares me a glance. "She may have seen a few things I did to someone who deserved it."

"I see," I murmur disapprovingly. The cult may be a horrible place, and she may have endured a lot, but if I know Jagger, the scene had to be horrific for her. Hell, it was probably horrific for anyone.

"Can you tell me your name?" I ask Issy carefully.

"You already know—" he begins, but I cut him off with a wave of my hand.

"Isabelle," she says, and it's barely above a whisper. I sit up a little straighter, however. Her voice tickles the edge of a memory, but I've treated many people, and sometimes their problems, voices, and quirks become something like déjà vu.

Balancing her mug on her knee, she uses a free hand to wipe at her tears, almost in an angry way. I'd love to know who she's angry at, but instead of asking that, I ask, "And are you having a boy or a girl?"

"We aren't going to find out," she responds, finally looking me in the eye.

"That's beautiful." I smile softly at her, but she doesn't return it. Instead, she looks back at her tea. "What's wrong? Why are you so upset that you're here?"

"You don't know what you've done," she begins in a small voice. And then she says it again, but louder this time. And then again. And then again, each time her voice grows in volume until she's screaming it.

I quickly get off my chair and dash to her, gripping her shoulders and demanding that she look at me. The tea falls to the floor, and the mug shatters as she finally cups her face, quiets her wailing, and sobs into her palms.

I glance at Jagger, and he looks at me. There's a wildness to his features, almost as if he doesn't know what to do. I suppose he doesn't. These emotions are foreign to him, and just like myself, we don't understand what she means.

"What do you mean 'you don't know what you've done'?" I ask her gently. I release my hold on her shoulders and kneel before her in the tea. I don't even care that my pants are getting wet. She's clearly having some sort of crisis, and at any moment, she could clam up. "Issy, what do you mean? What will the cult do?"

She drops her hands and shakes her head, hiccuping with emotion. "I don't know. There's no one there to lead it anymore. I don't know."

I breathe deep because with any luck, maybe the Temple will just disappear. Wither away into nothing. Maybe each and every one of them will go their separate ways now that there is no leader to govern over them.

"You shouldn't have taken me," she says angrily. If looks could kill, I'd be dead.

"You came on your own free will," Jagger mutters to her. "I didn't drag you out of there."

"I was in shock!" she hollers at him, finally facing her brother now. "How was I supposed to speak when you… when you—"

"Okay, okay, okay," I hush. I soothingly pat her knees to draw her attention back to me. "What would you like us to do?"

"Take me back," she says simply, almost matter-of-factly. It blows my mind, and I double blink at her. Does she…does she really think Jagger will let her go back?

"You—" I clear my throat, unsure if I heard her correctly. All I can think of is Sadie and how the very thought of the Temple nearly had her coming undone.

Now Jagger's sister wants to go back? It doesn't make sense. So I clarify, "You want to go back to the Temple?"

"Yes," she demands.

She makes to stand up to do just that, but Jagger sits her back down by applying pressure to her shoulder. "You are not going back, Issy. You're free, whether you want to see it or not."

"I am not free!" she yells at him.

He studies her, watches as she huffs and puffs and wipes away the fresh tears that slither down her cheeks. "Don't you see? They brainwashed you. Don't you get it? If you just give it time, you'll see that I'm right."

I watch as her jaw clamps shut and she whips her head to look out of the living room window, cutting us off completely with that simple gesture.

Well, shit.

"Can I talk to you for a second?" I say to Jagger, standing to full height. I try to keep the annoyance out of my tone, but I'm sad to say I'm not entirely successful.

I can tell he's reluctant to leave her side, but eventually, he nods, and we head to the kitchen together. It seems like ages ago that he was chasing me around this island, and now I'm taking a seat at it, possibly suggesting that he actually does as she asks and takes her back.

He paces the length of the island, and I allow it for a few seconds, resting my palms gently in my lap and trying like hell to have the patience I've never possessed. "Jagger," I call. He glances at me but continues to move restlessly. "I think you might need to consider that having her in the real world is doing more harm than good. Perhaps she's—"

Placing his hands on his hips, he turns to face me. "Don't you dare tell me she's too far gone."

"She might be," I hiss at him, because clearly he

doesn't see what I see. And honestly, we could have only scratched the surface of the damage going on inside of her. "Asking her to live what you consider a normal life isn't normal for her. All of this is foreign. You took away the only thing she knows. You damaged the only man that's ever loved her."

He laughs darkly and points at me. "Tyron does not love her."

I jab my finger in his direction, trying to be more stern with him. "In her mind, he does. Tell me, Jagger. What did you do to him? Hmm? What did she witness you doing to the only man that she believes loves her?"

His jaw flexes, but I don't miss the initial wince. "That's what I thought," I murmur when he doesn't say anything at all. I lower my hand back to my lap and sigh to relieve the tension in my shoulders. "What exactly is your plan here?"

"I was going to take her home and have her live with me." I can tell that he doesn't think that's going to work anymore, but I don't agree with him.

"If you're suggesting she stay here, I won't allow it," I begin with as much compassion as I can muster in this moment. I'm frustrated with him because he's seeing things only in the way he wants to see them. "She needs to stay at your place. You're the only one she knows, and if she has any chance of having any sort of comfort and security, it's going to be with her brother."

He hangs his head for a moment, then looks at me from under his lashes. "Even the brother who left her behind? Even the brother who didn't come back for her?"

I breathe deep and then let it out through my nose, trying like hell to let the sadness in his voice not affect me like it is. Damn him for having such a sway on me. "You need to talk to her. You both need to figure this out—the past, the present, and the future. It's the only way that you'll have a chance that she won't bolt for home at the first sign of your distraction."

He nods slowly, then straightens his shoulders as he comes to some sort of conclusion. "You're coming with us then."

"What?"

"To stay at my apartment. You're coming," he explains with zero room for discussion to be had.

"No," I say, adding a nervous chuckle. He can't be serious? I place a hand on my heart and continue, "This is your circus. Not mine."

He holds his arms out at his sides and gives a shrug. "You're mine, therefore, this makes it your problem too. Besides"—he crosses his arms over his chest—"you're best trained with how to deal with her."

"And what about my clients? What am I supposed to do with them? I have a job, Jagger. I cannot babysit your sister all day, every day."

He gives a little shrug. "Leave me with instructions."

I pinch the bridge of my nose. "You sound like an idiot right now," I mutter into my palm. He's infuriating, and I get why he's doing what he's doing and why he wants me to help, but I don't think it'll go well if it's just him and his sister. He's seeing this as a black-and-white situation, and it certainly isn't one. He will try to force her to behave in ways she doesn't believe in.

He crosses the distance to me, takes my fingers off my nose, and tips my face to meet his. "Please, darling." He kisses the tip of my nose in an uncharacteristic way for all things Jagger. Maybe there is hope for him if he can display this sort of gentleness with me. Perhaps he can provide the same for his sister. "Please help us. Please help me."

I search his face and find nothing but fear in his pleas. Unsure of what else I could possibly do for him other than what he's suggesting, because I do love him and I want what's best for him and his family, I nod against my better judgment.

I have a sinking feeling this is not going to end the way he wants it to. How can it, when she's already so damaged?

CHAPTER TWENTY-THREE
DOLLY STERLING

I STEP out of my front door and breathe in the crisp autumn air while wrapping my throw blanket tighter around me. Issy has only been here for the day, and it feels like it's been weeks. I just need a minute to feel something else battering against my skin, like the wind, instead of Issy's raw emotions. They went from tearful and afraid to outright angry in a matter of hours. She really doesn't want to be here, and truthfully, a hospital is a better setting for her than a stranger's or her brother's home. It'd be more familiar, more even ground than the weighing expectations of a long-lost brother and his therapist girlfriend.

I tip my head toward the dark sky and look at the stars. He's so damn determined to keep her with him, and he won't listen to me when I tell him this situation needs to change because it's doing her no good. It's traumatizing for her, and he refuses to see it.

We haven't moved her to his place yet. She's refusing to budge off my couch.

When I was cooking supper, a meal Issy outright declined, I asked Jagger if he'd contacted Rollo yet and told him what had gone down. At the very least the parts that don't incriminate him. He said he hadn't, and he wasn't going to. I guess Rollo had basically told him that the police weren't safe, and he's probably right. Savage Temple feels like it has eyes everywhere, even in my living room. After all, I can't imagine that he'd hand me a gun if he didn't believe the same, and Jagger probably picked up all those vibes at the station. He told me all about his time there when we were whispering in the kitchen over the stove.

The sound of tires on pavement pulls my attention to the street before me. Sadie's familiar red Volkswagen Beetle pulls up to the front of my house, and even in the darkness, I can see her unease. It's in the way her shoulders are bunched toward her neck.

I had been texting her all day, but she'd only responded to the first message, which was announcing Jagger's sister's arrival. I had told her everything else, but she hadn't responded, and until now, I thought it was because she didn't care. But perhaps it's because it was painful. A twinge of guilt settles in my heart about that. I should have protected Sadie from her past, but instead I brought her into it.

She sits there for a moment, staring at my house, and I allow her the time to adjust, knowing that someone she probably once played with is on the other side of the wall. Sometimes I wonder if Sadie has some guilt too, that she ran and left behind the other kids. Does it eat her alive like it does Jagger? Sadie may not have had siblings, but I'm sure all the kids were bonded in some way.

Finally, she opens the driver's door and steps out onto the road. When she pivots to face me, she has a tight expression on her face.

"Hey," I call to her while tightening the blanket around my shoulders. I can feel her emotion from here. Her fear has its own orbit.

She doesn't greet me back as she strides up my sidewalk to my front door. I breathe deep when she stops in front of me and crosses her arms uncomfortably over her chest. Her attention is strictly on my door. "Is Jagger still in there?"

I nod. "He talked about getting some groceries soon, buying things that she used to like, and then maybe trying to convince her again to go to his place. I have a feeling it will be a lot of bribing with candy, though." It almost feels like a last-ditch effort to win her favor, but I'm not going to mention that. There's no need to when we all know the truth.

"How's she doing?" Sadie asks, looking at my window that peeks into the living room. She won't be able to see Issy from her position, but I imagine she doesn't need to, and I get the vibe that she doesn't really want to. And that maybe she's just here for me and not to check on a friend she hasn't seen in years.

"Not well," I grumble. "I came out here after she had a fit with Jagger about having a glass of water. She's very resistant and insists we take her back."

"Are you going to?" she asks softly.

"I don't know," I breathe out. "This is harming her more than doing her any good. She's beyond stressed, and that's going to create more anger and blame, and she's going to direct it all at the person who saved her, at the person who abandoned her to begin with."

Sadie looks down at her feet, and it's then I realize how right I am that she also feels a little guilt and responsibility for this too.

I let her collect herself before I quietly ask, "Do you want to come in?"

She lifts her gaze to me, wipes away a tear, and quietly whispers, "Yeah."

"It'll be okay." I turn, open the front door, and together we stride into the warmth of my home. A bit of nervous energy overcomes me when Issy's angry gaze snaps from her brother's to Sadie's.

Jagger shifts uneasily from his spot on the couch next to Issy. He still holds the glass of water he's been trying to convince her to drink. "Sadie," he greets softly.

"Hey," she replies in the same volume.

Issy's pinched eyebrows shift in confusion as she studies Sadie. I'll give Sadie credit, she doesn't move an inch or fidget in any way. I would, and that just proves how strong Sadie really is. "Sadie who?" she demands to know.

"Probably the only Sadie you know," she answers back in a clear voice. She has more confidence in her stance and tone than I thought she would, and that makes me proud of her. "Or did you forget me?"

I can see the moment it hits Issy who exactly is standing before her, and instead of greeting an old friend like I'd hoped would happen, Issy snorts. "You fell far from the apple tree."

"What's that supposed to mean?" I ask as kindly as I can, because I know that term is generally used as a compliment, but in this case, it's clearly not.

"Look at her," Issy grumbles. She crosses her arms over her chest and glances away, dismissing her entirely. "She dresses like the devil's wife."

I take a look at my best friend, and honestly, I've never given a shit how she dresses. She's wearing black jeans that have holes all over them, a deep purple shirt with a low neckline, and a black leather jacket. Her piercings and numerous tattoos probably make her look more sinister than she actually is. She wears them for a reason: to disguise who she truly is.

Sadie narrows her eyes at the young woman. "I'm not the same girl that left. I've had to change who I was to hide where I came from. And honestly, Issy, you can hate me all you want, but all it's going to do is make me feel sorry for you."

"Why on earth would you feel sorry for me?" Issy hisses. She still refuses to look at Sadie.

"Because you have no idea that everything you've been told and how you were brought up is not how things are supposed to be. The Temple is not the right way of life, and you're so brainwashed that you can't even tell." She takes a step forward and kneels before Issy. "Let Jagger help you. Let him show you how life is supposed to be. Allow yourself the idea of freedom."

I'm surprised when Sadie touches Issy's knee. Sadie never shows that kind of affection with anyone but me, and she certainly doesn't show affection toward strangers.

I glance at Jagger and watch for a few seconds as he chews on the inside of his lip. He's not breathing as he waits for his sister's answer. I can tell he's hoping a familiar old friend will be able to sway her better than he ever could. I have to admit, I'm kind of hoping so too.

Slowly, Issy turns seething eyes on her, and my hope dashes the moment she growls, "Don't touch me."

Sadie removes her hand, hangs her head for a second, and stands back to full height. "It's too bad you can't see it, Is. But maybe with time, you will."

Issy's nails bite into the sleeves of her dress as she hisses, "I will never live an unclean life."

"Jesus," I mutter, trying like hell not to throw my hands in the air.

Jagger sighs, and Sadie simply shrugs. At this point, I honestly don't know if we will ever convince her not to lead a life mapped out for her by the Temple. I won't stop helping Jagger, though. I won't stop helping him try to save his sister, but I do need to convince him to change the location to somewhere more neutral. It's only going to benefit her, and hopefully he will see that with a few carefully picked out words when we get a chance to talk later tonight.

Handing me the glass of water, Jagger stands to his full height. His shoulders are slumped in defeat, and he scrubs at the back of his neck as he says, "I'm going to go get some groceries."

I pivot to face him more fully. "Do you need a ride?" His truck is in my driveway, but he doesn't look like he should be alone right now.

He shakes his head. "I'm going to drive there, clear my head a little."

"Are you sure?"

His answer is a soft kiss to my cheek, and then he's passing me and heading out the door. As soon as he's gone, the tension in the room kicks up a notch instead of easing like I assumed it would.

"Good," Issy says with fake cheer in her tone. "You two can take me back while he's gone."

I raise my eyebrows at her. "I'm not taking you anywhere."

With her hands on her hips, Sadie agrees. "Neither am I."

She sneers at us. "Both of you are going to hell."

"Probably," I grumble before heading to the kitchen to put the cup in the sink. She's clearly choosing dehydration over taking an offering from someone she deems unclean.

As soon as I reach my sink, I place my hands on either side of cold metal and bow my head. I have no idea how I'm going to find the strength to be there for Sadie and Jagger when I'm already at my wit's end. Helping her recover will take years, not months. Un-brainwashing her isn't going to be overnight like Jagger wants and Sadie expects. How do I dash their hope when I give them an estimate on how long this could take and that maybe, just maybe, she will never have normal beliefs, that she could be sicker than even I realize, and that she could be gone from them forever?

I hold my breath for ten seconds and release it slowly, hoping to rid the bad energy from my body if not from my home. It works a little, but not well enough.

I hear a few footsteps behind me, and just as I'm about to turn and greet who I think is Sadie with a ready excuse that I need a minute, something hits me on the side of my head.

Immediately, I fall to the ground, and the world goes dark around me.

CHAPTER TWENTY-FOUR
JAGGER VALENTINE

DO I GET HER CANDY? I ask myself as I stand near the checkout counter, arms full of random things most kids like. I know she's not a kid anymore, but she once was, and she once wanted all of these things. I still remember that day clearly—the day my father punished us for her being given candy. Would it bring back that memory if I presented it to her? Or would it sway her to listen to me?

"Are you ready, sir?" the elderly female cashier asks.

"Yeah." I'm next in line and hadn't realized the man in front of me was gone while I contemplated what my sister might like. Without thinking any further, I grab a chocolate candy bar and take the few steps to the belt where I unload my arms.

The cashier chuckles as a box of crackers tumbles to the floor. I quickly snatch it as she says, "How many littles do you have at home?"

I scowl as I toss the box back on the belt. She starts scanning my items. "Excuse me?"

She looks at me with her dull, motherly blue eyes, slightly confused. "Oh, sorry, dear. I figured you had kids. My grandbabies enjoy these snacks, is all. I thought…never mind."

Stuffing my hands in my pockets, I wait for the total

to be displayed before I pull out my wallet and hand over cash for what I hope is some resemblance of a meal for Issy.

As she bags my groceries, she starts to talk about her grandchildren, but I pay no attention to it. My mind is elsewhere—on my sister, Dolly, and Sadie; how they're getting along and if Sadie managed to convince her that she's in the right place. She has to see reason eventually. She has to know that we mean her no harm. This is the best choice for her, and I'm going to convince her of that if it's the last thing I do. I love my sister, and I need her to be okay. I don't know what I'm going to do if she's not, if she can't accept a normal way of life.

Finally, she finishes by placing the candy bar in the bag, and I grab my groceries and head out the door. It's still windy, and the breeze immediately pushes against me as soon as I step outside. I ignore it and stride as fast as I can to my car, wanting to get back to my sister and my girl just in case they need me.

I open the passenger door of my truck and drop the groceries on the seat, and then head around to the driver's side. As soon as I'm inside, I start the engine, and at the same time, my phone begins to ring.

It takes me a minute to slip it out of my pocket, but when I do, Dolly's name pops up along with her picture. I answer it right away. "Hey, darling," I murmur sweetly, because after all, she's doing a lot for me. "I'm still at the store. Do you need something?"

"Darling?" A male chuckle comes through, but it's weak and nasally, as if he has a stuffy nose. I, however, would know that voice anywhere, despite that.

"Tyron? You're alive. I wasn't sure anyone would find you in time." My words may be carefree, but my heart slams against my ribs. If he has Dolly's phone, then he has Dolly. How did he get her? Did the Temple find out where Dolly lived? Did they make the connection? Did someone they know see us come to her house? Questions reel in my head at a rapid pace.

"Did you forget that we have doctors?" he says softly, as if he doesn't have the energy to put a rude lilt to it.

I did forget about the doctors. They have several in their back pocket who make visits specifically for Temple people. We go to them if it's just germs and infections, but if it's something more serious, something we don't want made public, they would come to Savage Temple.

"Did they get your balls put back together?" I jab, even though I'm so terrified that a fine sweat breaks out on my back. How the fuck am I going to save Dolly? Does he have my sister too? I can't imagine he doesn't. Is she being punished? Fuck...

"I don't think you know how much you're going to pay for that, Jagger," he draws out. There's pleasure in his tone, and all it does is add an abundance of fear.

"What is your plan, Tyron?"

"Well, since I have two important women in your life, one from the present and one from the past, I may have to think of something genius."

"Let my sister and Dolly go, asshole. It's me you want anyway."

"Oh, I don't have your sister. There's no 'having' your sister when she's the one who brought them here. I have to say, I'm surprised she was able to knock out two women, drag them into one of their cars, and bring them to the property all on her own. It's a good thing that baby of mine isn't too large, or that would have been impossible for her."

My heart skips a beat. My sister would never betray me. "You're lying."

"I'm not." He goes into a mild coughing fit and then curses against pain. "I'm not the one who organized any of this, Jagger. I'm not the one in charge since your father died, even though you thought otherwise. I am not king. She is."

My pulse rings in my ears, and my hand holding my phone begins to shake. "You're lying!"

"Ask her yourself."

"You're lying!" I shout again, slamming my palm against the steering wheel.

"He's not, Jagger," my sister says, and I freeze, because that voice...it belongs to that little girl I left behind. It's no longer womanly, but instead, it's childlike. I hadn't realized he passed the phone. I hadn't realized...

What the fuck is happening? Why does she sound like a child?

A chill runs through my veins at the way her pitch slithers down my spine. That childlike voice holds things I don't want to contemplate, things I cannot imagine.

I squeeze the steering wheel as tight as I can. "What are you doing, Issy?" I'm aware of how meek my tone sounds, even as deep as it is.

"You have a choice here," she begins, ignoring my question with an air of authority. In the background, I can hear sobbing, and I just know without a doubt that one of those sobbers is Dolly. "If you want to save Sadie and your Dolly, you'll give me something."

"And what is that?"

"You come back to Savage Temple. You reinsert yourself into our way of life, and we make you clean once more." A toddler giggle follows.

"No," I immediately say. Even though my sister may be in charge, I won't go back there. I did everything to escape.

"Then I'll kill them," she says simply. "I should kill them anyway for what you did to Tyron, but you can take that punishment as it should be. What's your choice, big brother? Return into the fold, or bury Sadie and Dolly?"

I snarl into the phone.

"Oh, Jagger," she murmurs with disappointment. "Please come home to me."

"What happened to you?" I whisper, completely dumbfounded.

There are two breaths before she says, "Oh! We could play with my tea set. I kept it just for you." There's another pause before she continues, "Now choose, brother of mine. You have until sunrise. And Jagger? Come alone. Leave the bestie at home."

And then she's gone.

CHAPTER TWENTY-FIVE
DOLLY STERLING

SHE LOOKS CHILLINGLY NO-NONSENSE when she hangs up on Jagger. No. A child who is in charge of an empire. A child playing queen. No longer that crying woman on my living room couch, Issy is at home while barking orders and expecting people to listen, while at the same time, having reverted back to a ten-year-old girl. How long has she been in charge of Savage Temple to have that amount of confidence? And why do they listen to her when she's clearly...broken? And another thing... why didn't she display this other personality in my home?

Clearly she had some sort of snap since the trauma of whatever Jagger did to get her out. Or maybe the trauma of being ripped from her home. Or maybe this existed, and it's only being brought out to the light whenever she's under great stress.

I don't have answers to these questions, but as someone who professionally dives into people's brains, Issy may be one of those cases when they're too far gone to truly help, too damaged to know right from wrong. Most of the time those people develop disorders that put them in psych wards, and I'd be the first one to shove her in one. Perhaps dissociative identity disorder? For some odd reason, her subconscious believes she's safer as a child than as an adult. It's creepy as hell, but I'm honestly not surprised something is mentally wrong with her.

Issy turns her gaze upon Sadie and me, both of us bound by our wrists that are strapped to the headboard spokes on a bed. The bed is inside a decent-sized room with striped pink and purple wallpaper.

Jagger's sister wrinkles her nose when she looks at Sadie's bright red welt on top of her forehead where she had clearly hit her to knock her out. The side of my head still thumps to the beat of my heart from where she had hit me, too.

I don't remember the car ride over. I don't even remember getting on the property. I just remember waking on this bed with Issy fitting us comfortably on the mattress, almost like we were dolls. The dresses she had put us in before we even woke resemble doll clothes as well, frilly with floral patterns. And then as my hearing returned, I listened to her talk in the same child-like voice to a man at the foot of my bed named Tyron. He's in a wheelchair without pants, wearing some sort of diaper bandage thing over his lower region. Right now, he holds a giant ice pack to it.

I have very little interest in why his lower half is clearly injured, and instead, I just want to stay the hell away from him. The way he's looking at me and Sadie makes my skin crawl. If there was such a thing as undressing someone with their eyes…

"He should be here soon," Issy says to him while placing my phone at the foot of the bed. She then turns to him and pecks him on the cheek. Once she rights herself, she opens the adjacent closet door, lifts a black leather box from atop the shelf, and sets it on the end of the bed. Gracefully, she opens the lid and gently pulls out a pistol, resting it on the edge of the bed by my phone. "Any funny business and you shoot them. Okay, Daddy?"

Sadie immediately starts gagging, and not the fake kind. I have to admit, I'm disgusted too, but I know knowledge is on my side. I know how mentally ill she is, and for him to go along with it, to almost look at her adoringly because of it, is telling to this relationship.

She plays the child because of her illness, and he likes children. That's plainly obvious as I observe him watching her stride out of the room. And then it hits me…

Shook, I glance at Sadie. "He's your father?" I see the resemblance in the set of the eyes and in the shape of the mouths.

She turns dark, glaring eyes toward Tyron, who now stares at her plainly. "He's just the bastard that gave his sperm to my mother."

"That's no way to talk to your father," Tyron mutters. There's a fine sheen of sweat on his forehead, and his skin is pale, almost as though he has a fever. He adjusts his hand on the ice, and the cubes rattle inside the plastic bag that contains them.

What the hell happened to this guy? Did someone castrate him? *Whoever did it had done the world a favor,* I think to myself as he turns his interested expression to me.

"Don't. Don't even look at her," Sadie growls at him.

Tyron places the bag of ice at the foot of the bed next to my phone and then picks up the pistol, weighing it in his hands. "You know," he says weakly into the room. "I often fantasized about what I'd do to you when you returned home. How I'd make you pay, what I'd do to break you into nothing but a rambling mess. And now you're here. And you brought a dolly with you. How sweet."

He places the gun on his adult diaper bandage and slowly wheels in my direction, passing by the window until he comes to rest by my waist. His eyes scan my body, and his tongue darts out to moisten his bottom lip in what I perceive as sickening excitement.

"Stay the fuck away from her," Sadie threatens. The rope around her wrists strains as she tugs, jostling the mattress underneath us.

"You do look like a doll, don't you? What a coincidence that your name is Dolly. Tell me, Dolly? Do you know what your lover did to me?"

"I don't particularly care," I say back, and it's not as confident as I want it to be. I don't feel safe next to him, and it has nothing to do with the gun in his lap. Whatever he has in mind, I much prefer the gun anyway.

"The doctors tell me I'll never be able to have children again," he mutters, reaching and touching my cheek. I whip my face away from his hand, but he persists, giving me no option but to endure when I run out of length in my neck to get away from him.

"Pity," Sadie spits.

"I wonder what Jagger would do if I made you a rambling mess instead of Sadie and sent you on your way, damaged and broken back into the real world. Hmm?" He runs his thumb over my bottom lip, and I have half a mind to bite it off. But then I remember that I'm not the only one in this room, and my actions may have consequences for Sadie. So I endure, holding back the bile rising in my throat.

He looks at my knees where the edge of my doll dress lies, and he eagerly reaches for it as some kind of idea hits him.

"Don't touch her!" Sadie threatens again, but it falls on deaf ears just as before.

"What if I shoved my gun so far up that pussy and fired at will? That way we both won't have children," he goes on. He lifts the dress ever-so-slowly, and I start to tremble while Sadie starts huffing and puffing, probably going through her own personal hell right now. I get the feeling his ease and leisureliness are on purpose.

He continues to lift it until it's around my waist.

"Please stop," I beg as he leans back and observes my lower half.

"Well, would you look at that?" he murmurs lovingly. "She left your underwear off, just for me." He turns a weak grin toward me, his face still sickly pale and even worse now that he's up close. "She knows what I like, you know. She's a good girl like that."

"Fuck you," I whisper when he wraps his hand around his gun's hilt. And then I find some strength within and yell, "Fuck you!"

He brings the gun to the juncture of my thigh. He points the gun at my pussy, placing his finger on the trigger, and I squeeze my eyes shut, waiting for the pain. But it never comes. The next thing I hear is a crack, a thump, an oof, and a thunderous clatter.

My eyes fly open, and I watch as Sadie straddles her father in the wheelchair, takes the splintered spoke that her wrists were once tied to, and jams it into his eye. He doesn't have time to react, he doesn't even scream. One minute he's flailing for balance in his wheelchair and the next, he has a wood rod sticking out of his eye. His limbs drop and dangle lifelessly at the sides of the wheels.

Thump, thump, thump. My heart beats loud in my ears.

Sadie falls silent for a moment until she lets out a loud sob. She grabs the spoke, yanks it out of his eye, and rams it into his chest. Blood squirts here and there, sprinkling on Sadie's and my legs.

Thump, thump, thump.

"Hey," I whisper as she begins to sob once more. She climbs off of her father's lap, pushes him away on the chair's wheels, and slumps down to the floor. She covers her face with her bloody hands and cries openly into her palms.

"Sadie," I call again, trying to keep my voice down, but I can already hear footsteps coming down the hall. I angle my body so I can see over the bed a little better. The gun had fallen right next to her hip, so I whisper a little louder, "Sadie! Grab the gun! She's coming!"

She doesn't hear me, probably too absorbed in herself from trauma, and my heart beats rapidly in my chest as I swivel my gaze back toward the door. What will Issy do once she sees that her father figure and lover is dead? How will she react? How doomed are we?

"Sadie," I try hissing again, but it's too late.

"What is going on in h—" Issy asks as she enters the door with her hands on her hips. She takes in the scene with a ten-year-old dumbfounded expression and whispers, "Daddy?" as soon as her eyes land on the spoke sticking out of Tyron's chest.

"Issy," I say clearly, tugging on my wrists as her gaze turns angry and fixates on the only person who could have done that to her man. "Issy, I need you to listen to me."

But she doesn't. Instead, she marches into the room with her hands fisted on her side, heads to the leather box where she left it, and lifts another gun from inside.

"Sadie!" I shout, the sound deafening to my own ears. I whip my head in Sadie's direction just as she lowers her hands to my voice, and then a gun fires and there's a hole in her forehead. Her brains splatter on the wall behind her.

Thump, thump, thump.

The only thing I hear after that is the screaming of my own voice echoing in my ears.

Issy places the gun back inside the box as if she didn't just murder someone she knows, probably once loved and admired. Then she heads to Tyron and grasps the handles of his wheelchair. Over my screaming I can clearly hear her say, "Let's go clean you up, Daddy."

And then she wheels him away, leaving me with what's left of my best friend and what's left of me.

CHAPTER TWENTY-SIX
JAGGER VALENTINE

I STAND before my sister's house, hours after she called. Sunrise is behind me, the sun's rays glinting against the frost of every blade of grass. I don't even remember the last time I slept. I stand there, reading Blake's text message for the thousandth time, not knowing if I'll ever actually talk to him again.

BLAKE

You don't have to do it this way. There are other ways. There has to be other ways!

ME

There isn't.

BLAKE

For fuck's sake, Jagger! I hope you're not making a mistake you can't live with!

Please don't do this, Jag. Please.

I didn't respond after that. Instead, I just replay his last words in my head, trying not to let them sink in, but they linger anyway. I can't go back, I can't listen to him. I have to save Dolly, if it's not too late already.

The entire way here, I couldn't stop imagining what they were doing to her, how they were mistreating her, and what she'd be like once I found her and they released her. I know this place, I know these people, and I know how fucked up they are. What am I going to do if the woman I love is harmed?

Love. Love?

I scowl, and then it slowly relaxes off my face. I do. I fucking love that woman, and if I have to trade places with her, if I have to do what I'm about to do to save her life, I'm going to. I'm going to put her life above mine, because she's worth it. Because I need her to live, I need her alive, and I need her to keep breathing and be sane and be everything that makes her her. I have to know that out of this entire situation, she'll remain Dolly.

Pocketing my phone, I step fully up to the door. There are people I recognize beside the door, boarding up the bay window I shattered. From the looks of it, they're almost done. It doesn't matter, they pretend I don't exist anyway. To them, I'm unclean, and simply talking to me will make them unclean too.

I don't bother knocking. I simply turn the knob and step into the home. Immediately I smell two things: copper and baked sugar. The two together do not mix well. It's thick in the air, making my stomach twist more than it already is.

The house is dark, and it takes me a minute to adjust to the lack of light. And then I see it. Or him, for that matter.

Sitting in the dining room in a wheelchair is Tyron. But he's not alive. He can't be, not with a wooden stake sticking out of his chest.

I simply blink at his corpse, unsure of what to make of it, but I don't have long to dwell on it because my sister strides around the corner with a plate full of chocolate chip cookies in one hand and a glass of milk in the other. She smiles brightly at me, sets them down on the table, and travels back to the wall to flick on the dining room lights.

I take in the scene before me: my sister's bright and young smile, Tyron's blood all over his face and down his shirt, and the hospitable snacks on the table. She walks over to Tyron and wheels him up to the side of the table, and then gestures for me to sit next to him. "You're just in time for snack time," she says cheerfully. She's using that same little girl voice she had on the phone.

Slowly, as if they're not my own feet, I make my way toward the table, a little numb inside. "Um." I clear my throat and try not to look too hard at Tyron. Though I enjoy the fact that he's dead, I don't think my sister would take too kindly to me pointing it out. "Did you make this just for me?"

I tug back a chair and take a seat, still having a sort of out-of-body experience. The smell of copper is thicker here, and it's then that I realize it's blood that I'm smelling. I know the smell of blood and had once celebrated it, but today it makes me sick. I want Tyron dead, but I question...how did he die, and what did my sister do to the person who killed him?

My stomach rolls, and I want nothing more than to ask my sister about it, but I have to play this by her rules. Everything that happens from here on out will be by her rules because she's clearly delusional. Sick. Twisted. So fucked up that I don't even know who I'm looking at: the devil or the little girl I left behind.

What the hell happened to her after I left? Guilt rides me hard. This, all of this, is my fault.

She takes a seat across from me, fluffing out her dress and scooting it under her ass before she sits. "Yes, brother. Of course. I was so excited that you were coming that I whipped up your favorite." She giggles as she grabs a cookie. "It's Mother's recipe, you know. Go on, grab one, silly!"

I wipe a hand over my mouth, in utter disbelief right now, but I do as she asks and grab a cookie.

"The milk is for you too," she whispers conspiratorially, cupping her hand around the side of her mouth. "I remember how much you like to dunk them."

I swallow thickly and grab the glass of milk, sliding it in my direction. The milk jostles inside, but it doesn't spill over. I then set my cookie next to it, hoping that the act itself is enough to satisfy her.

"Um," I begin, finally looking at Tyron. He has a gaping hole where his eye was, and I can't help but take in every detail, including the wooden slivers embedded in the flesh. "About Tyron…"

"He's dead," she states matter-of-factly with a curt nod.

I place my hands on my thighs and rub my sweating palms against my jeans. "Oh, so you noticed?"

She nods like a bobblehead toy. "His daughter killed him, and then I killed her. But he'll be fine." She leans over and brushes her fingertips lovingly over his arm. "I'll fix him up just like I did when you broke my Barbies. Remember?"

"Yeah," I murmur.

"I love him," she declares with a bright and wide smile. "We'll have a baby, and he can sit here and watch while I raise him or her." She leans a little closer to him and rests her cheek on his shoulder. "Won't that be lovely, Daddy?"

I shift uncomfortably. I don't think this can get any more fucked up than it already is. "Issy, where's Dolly?"

She scowls and then sits straight in her seat once more. "That witch is still in Sadie's bed."

"Unharmed?"

Her brows pinch together, as if she doesn't know the answer to that. "As far as I know."

I breathe a sigh of relief. "Where's Sadie?"

"I killed her, remember?" she answers simply. "I killed her next to Dolly, and now she won't be a problem anymore."

I swallow with difficulty and try not to let it show that that news devastates me. Rollo…oh god, Rollo is going to be fucking destroyed. And Dolly? Fuck. If she truly did see her death, Dolly is going to be so fucked up when she leaves here. I have to get her out of here soon. "What about Dolly, Is? Can I see her?"

She juts her chin back as if avoiding a physical slap. "Why would you want to see Dolly? Can't that wait? You're here for me, not for her."

How do I tell her that she's the love of my life? I can't. My sister is unstable, and she won't take that news well. What the fuck am I going to do? "I'd like to say goodbye is all. And then you have me. All to yourself, you have me, once we let her go."

She grabs a piece of her hair and starts twirling it around her fingers, weaving and whirling. "You know, I'd been trying to get Dolly separated from you for a long time so that you could come home."

"What do you mean?"

"I spied on you once I learned you were alive. I don't like her, you know. She was obsessed with you, she would have broken your heart."

I ignore how wrong she is and refocus her attention. I lean across the table and grab her hand. It doesn't even feel like a hand. It feels like the paw of a demon. "How were you going to separate Dolly from me?"

She covers her mouth with her free hand and giggles like a toddler. It makes me uncomfortable as hell, sending goose bumps across my shoulder blades, but she answers, "At first I followed her around to see where she goes. She goes the same places all day long. And then I'd been trying to get into her as a client, been calling and calling, but she always says she's full."

I blink at her, realizing now that my sister was that person. "And what would you have done once you met with her?"

She blinks twice at me, as if it should be obvious. "Well, kill her, of course. She doesn't love you. Not like I love you. But you're too afraid of this place to know that I still love you lots. Even when I broke you out of jail to show you that I was in charge now, you still didn't come to live with me. Instead, you marched in here and damaged Daddy." She looks sadly at Tyron's crotch, then her mood flips back to happy once more, and she adds, "But you're here now, so it doesn't matter."

I gently rub my thumb over the back of my sister's hand and fight like hell to hold back tears. With a clogged throat, I ask her, "Issy, what happened to you after I left? Do you remember that day? When I ran away?"

She nods as if it were no big deal.

"What happened? What did Father do?"

Immediately, her face contorts to anger, and a deep voice I don't recognize emits loudly from her throat. "We don't talk about that!" She hits herself in the head a few times as hard as her fists can. "No! No! We don't talk about that!"

My spine hits the back of my chair in utter shock. I release her hand immediately and grip the edge of my seat, wondering for the hundredth time…what the fuck is happening?

"Issy?" I whisper, unsure if I'm actually talking to my sister or someone else entirely. She may be sitting there, but this isn't her. I don't know who this is.

With the flip of a switch, Issy's face returns to the

normal childish glee. "What did you do when you left, Jagger? Did you see the world like you always wanted to?"

A tear falls from my eye, and I don't bother wiping it away. She doesn't notice it at all, she doesn't see how devastated I am. "Yes. Yes, I did."

"That's good," she says. She reaches for a cookie and takes a generous bite of it, chewing thoughtfully. I give her a few minutes while I collect myself.

"Issy? We need to let Dolly go, okay? Can you take me to her? Let's let her go and begin our new life, okay?"

"Sure!" she says brightly. Abruptly, she stands up, grabs another cookie, and skips around Tyron.

My chair scrapes against the floor, and I follow her down the hall of the house, my pulse thundering in my veins.

CHAPTER TWENTY-SEVEN
DOLLY STERLING

SILENT TEARS TRACE my cheeks as footsteps once again travel down the hallway. There are two sets this time, but I don't have it in me for another attack of any kind. I don't give a shit anymore what happens next, not after all this.

Sadie still sits against the wall, her head lulled to the side while bits of bone, brain, and blood drip down the paint. There's a stench to it, one I've never smelled before, and it makes my stomach roll.

My best friend...she's gone. What gave her life was blown out the back of her head in the blink of an eye by some crazy, delusional woman. I blink through tears as I stare up at the ceiling's bubbled texture. I'll never hear her voice again, never see her smile. She'll never hug me and tell me everything will be okay even though the contact is almost painful for her. *Was*. It *was* painful for her, past tense.

A sob racks my body. My friend is gone forever, and there wasn't a damn thing I could do to save her life. This is my fault. I brought her to my house, I showed Issy that she was still alive, and Issy took us both. If I hadn't told or even suggested that Sadie come to my house, she'd still be alive.

"Oh Dolly," that child-bitch calls sweetly from my doorway.

I swivel my gaze to her and pin her with a glare, but she's not alone. I know the man with her, but instead of my heart skipping with joy, it fills with dread.

Jagger towers over her from behind, and I cry for a whole new reason now. He's come to save me, to set me free, to get me out of the fucking room. But I know, deep down, he's not coming with. He's going to stay. I can see it in the set of his jaw, and that's when the dread settles.

The rest of his expression is relieved when he surveys me and finds me unharmed, but it quickly turns into a mask when his attention slides to Sadie's corpse. I squeeze my eyes shut for a second, forcing all the tears out from inside my eyelids so my vision isn't blurry. They stream down my face in hot, salty trails.

When I open them, I croak, "She's delusional, Jagger." How do I explain to him that she's off her rocker, that there's no fixing her? How do I tell him his sister is too far gone and if we both want to live, he has to do something about it?

But that's his sister, and I'm the girl he practically just met. He loves her and me? What he feels for me is likely second to how he feels for her. He's spent a decade of guilt leaving behind the only person he's ever loved, and now he's here. Now, he has to choose.

My heart sinks as I realize that he likely won't choose me. He'll assume the guilt of what his sister has become and try to care for her as best he can, because it'll soothe the guilt itself. He won't choose me. He'll choose her because he's a good guy. Whether he wants to believe it or not, there is a good man inside him.

"I don't even know what that word means," Issy grumbles, crossing her arms over her chest and pouting like the child she is.

"You're sick," I tell her as calmly as I can. My voice shakes anyway. "You need help, more than your people can give you, more than Jagger can give you, and more than even I can give you. You need help, Isabelle, and no one can take that first step but you. You need a hospital and a team of doctors. Let me take you there, let me get you help."

Her face contorts into rage, and although her arms are crossed, her nails bite deeply into the skin of her arms, drawing blood. Her voice is almost demonic as she screams, "I'm not leaving! Don't make me kill you!"

A chill runs down my spine, and I try to breathe calmly through my flared nostrils. In the blink of an eye, her face relaxes back to the doe-eyed innocent child.

She peeks over her shoulder, lovingly gazing upon her brother. "Here she is, Jag."

He clears his throat, his shoulders stiff and his face tense. "Issy, let's send her on her way like you told me you would."

Jagger makes a move to go around her and come into the room to do just that, but she puts a hand on his chest. "But you have a punishment first, remember?"

"You said nothing about a punishment," he mutters as evenly as he can. That word…I know how that word affects him, bringing about great and horrible memories, but he's hiding it well.

She slaps his chest playfully. "You're unclean. We have to clean you first before you can be one of us again."

He peeks at me, but only for a second. He must feel my unease because we both know that his cleaning is going to involve me.

"Issy…" It's almost a plea, the way it comes out of his mouth.

"Oh, it won't be so bad," she says cheerfully, turning

back to face me. She points at me, and my fear spikes up a notch. "All you have to do is pick up the gun."

"And then what?"

I swear to God her eyes sparkle with glee. "Kill her, of course."

Shit. I swallow thickly.

Jagger's and my gaze meet, and it's then and there I know he for certain has to choose. There is no doubt in my mind now because she spoke it into existence. *Kill me,* she told him. Now he really does have to pick. Me or her. Family or lover. It's an impossible choice, and truth be told, if roles were reversed and I had a sister who was mentally sick, a sister I had tremendous guilt over for her mental illness, I'd probably pick her too. She'd need me, I'd be the only person she'd have left.

"That's not part of the deal you made with me, Is," he says with as much authority as he can muster. His eyes never leave me, almost as though he's trying to communicate with me, but I don't know what he's trying to say. Neither of us have been in stressful situations together. I don't know his cues.

It doesn't matter anyway. I'll be gone in a second, just like Sadie. There will be nothing left to contemplate.

There's a youthful patience in Issy's tone as she responds to her brother. "You know the rules, Jagger. Father made sure we knew the rules. Just because you've been gone doesn't mean they don't affect you. Now pick up the gun, silly!"

His throat bobs when his attention swivels from mine to the daunting gun at my feet. I can tell he's almost numb as he crosses the short distance to the end of the bed and robotically picks it up. He stares at it like he's never seen one before, and I know for a fact that he has. It's what he's about to do, the killing machine that he is. He's going to murder someone in the name of family.

"It's okay," I whisper to him. I sniff back the tears and relax my shoulders as I resign myself to my fate. "It's okay, Jag," I tell him again, and this time he looks at me from under his lashes.

"Darling," he mouths, his face contorting in pain.

I give him a reassuring nod. "She needs you. Promise me you'll help her. Promise me you'll keep her under control." Because we both know a girl like this, in this state, is dangerous. Hell, look at her now.

He closes his eyes, and his hands begin to tremble. I know this pains him, but I also know he'll live through it. Jagger is many things, and strong is certainly one of them. He's been through so much, survived so much, and he will survive this too. I have every ounce of my faith in that.

He raises the gun and points it at me, and when he opens his eyes, there's such agony in his expression that it breaks my heart. My pulse roars in my ears, but my body is completely relaxed as he levels it with my head, right where Sadie had been shot.

Issy giggles and claps her hands with excitement. "Do it! Do it, big brother!"

"Darling," he mouths to me, and I know if sound had come out, it'd be laced with the agony that's on his face.

"Come on, Jag!" she continues. "Right between the eyes! And when you're done, we can sit her right next to Daddy at the table. She'll still be with us, and you won't have to be sad!"

Moisture gathers in his eyes, and his lips pinch together, and I know it's to keep them from wobbling.

"I love you," I whisper to him.

"Do it, do it, do it," she chants. "Do it, Do—"

In the blink of an eye, Jagger swivels. The gun goes off in the next second. Issy's head jolts backward, slamming into the doorjamb. Her body then leans forward before she falls to a heap on the floor.

CHAPTER TWENTY-EIGHT
JAGGER VALENTINE

ALL I CAN HEAR IS the gunshot ringing in my ears. There's blood pooling around my sister's body, blood from blowing her head wide open, and what I feel inside is a shock to me. It's not what I expected.

The trembling in my fingers eases, and my pulse slows to a more even rhythm as I come to terms with the fact that she's dead. That it's over. That she can't hurt anyone else, and she certainly can't hurt Dolly.

Setting the gun down, I slowly shift to face the woman I chose. Her expression is wide and afraid, and her chest heaves with every breath. I head to the side of the bed that Sadie's body isn't on, kneel onto the mattress, and start to untie the ropes. I recognize the knots, I had taught them to Issy myself when we were bored.

Issy. My sister. Dead.

I glance back at her body as soon as Dolly's free and accept the embrace as Dolly wraps her arms around my neck and sobs into my shoulder. "Why did you choose me?" she asks through sobs. "She's your sister!"

I pull her away and press a gentle kiss to her forehead, then I look into her eyes as I clearly state, "My sister died the day I left here. That wasn't my sister, do you hear me?" I wipe away a few of her tears with my thumbs. "No one could have brought my sister back. Not even God himself."

She searches my gaze as a loud pounding begins at the home's front door. "Isabelle?" a man shouts from outside.

"Who is that?" Dolly asks in a fast whisper. Her entire body tenses, and I know that today is going to be the worst day of her life. She's going to remember everything my sister did and everything I might have to do just to get her out of here.

"Members of Savage Temple," I whisper back. I grab her hand and help her off the bed. "Come on. We have to leave right now."

She hops off the bed with my help, and we step over my sister's body before rushing down the hall. The pounding continues at the front door, the men calling from the other side. It's unlocked. At any moment they'll say screw our privacy tradition and enter to find the shit show we are leaving behind.

I make a left at the dining room, and I tug her along as we head toward the back door. As quietly as I can, I yank it open, and we enter the backyard. I look this way and that, and my heart eases when I realize that no one is up yet. We just have to get by whoever is at the front door and race to my car to get the fuck out of here. Then…then we will be safe. Or as safe as possible until I get my girl out of this town—this state—and find a place for us to hide from the Temple.

We start running as soon as we both notice that the coast is clear, and the frosted grass crunches under our feet. Our breaths fan out in front of us and then trail behind as we leave the mist cloud in our dust. I tug her along, forcing her to keep up with me as we pass houses and buildings. My car is parked at my father's house, and it's not too far ahead. If we push a little faster, we can be off the property in less than a minute.

I skid to a stop just before the corner of a house so that I can peek around it, but Dolly's legs keep going, and she flails out into the open, her hand straining against mine until she's tumbling forward.

I curse under my breath, reaching for her, but someone else's arms get to her first. This new man in a plaid long-sleeve shirt hoists her off the ground and tugs her back to his chest. A split second later, a kitchen knife is angled at her throat.

Adrenaline spikes in my veins, making it hard to breathe normally, as I take in the man's face. I recognize him. He's aged, but I remember his name: Joseph. And by the look in his eyes, he recognizes me too. Perhaps he knew I was going to be here, or perhaps my sister told everyone, but he doesn't look happy about it.

"Trying to escape so soon?" his gravelly, aged voice growls. His skin is like leather, and his wrinkles are deep. There's a hunch between his shoulders, but by the way he holds Dolly, I can tell he still has all of his strength.

The shadow of the house holds me at bay while the sun glints on the side of his summer-kissed face. What should I do? I meet Dolly's eyes and find hers wide and afraid yet again. Her fingers are digging into the old man's arms, but if he feels any pain, he isn't letting on. The knife is dangerously close to cutting her, so tackling them is out of the question.

"Move an inch, and she's dead."

"What do you want me to do, then?" I snarl at him.

"You're going to go into your father's house, and you're going to sit there while we discuss what to do with you. And this little lady here? She's going to come with me." He leans his mouth next to her ear. "Say goodbye now. You won't be seeing him again."

She may not know it, but I certainly do. That was a death threat for her and for me. I know he won't hesitate to kill her, and I know he'll enjoy punishing me in the process. They all will, especially when the news travels about Issy being dead.

"Over my dead body," I bark, and I take a step in their direction.

The blade of the kitchen knife moves just an inch and nicks her skin. I come to a halt as she angles her face away and hisses. Blood starts dribbling down her neck, and I flex and unflex my fists. He wasn't lying, and now I'm out of ideas.

"Did you think I was joking, Jagger?" the old man murmurs in triumph.

I open my mouth to respond but an arm sticks out from beyond the corner of the house from the old man's left, and a gun is now aimed at his temple. "Do *you* think I'm joking?" a familiar voice asks.

"Rollo?" Dolly whispers, and she cranes her eyes to see him.

I step out of the shadows and toward them a little further, indeed finding Rollo there. He's dressed in his cop uniform and has on his bulletproof vest, but it's his face that gets me. It's the expression of pure rage. "Put down the fucking knife," Rollo growls in warning. "I have no problems shooting all of you fuckwads."

I've never heard Rollo sound so dangerous. I didn't even know it was possible for that tone to come out of his mouth, but it's threatening enough that the man doesn't think about it long. He opens his hand, and the knife falls to the grass.

As soon as the knife thumps at his feet, a swarm of cops rushes past Joseph and heads deeper onto Temple property. Rollo marches forward, grabs Joseph's arms away from Dolly, and wrenches them behind his back. The sound of clicking handcuffs quickly follows. A policewoman jerks the old man away from Dolly and Rollo and starts marching him away while reading him his rights.

Dolly takes the opportunity of freedom to rush into my arms, and I embrace her, holding her face close to my neck and tucking her into my body. I kiss the top of her head as Rollo places one hand on his hip.

"So this is home, huh?" he asks me, looking around. He looks disgusted.

"This was never home," I grumble.

Dolly, she's my home. She's where I've always been meant to be. I just need to find a way to tell her that. But not now, not with everything that's happened. She isn't like me. She needs time to process.

"Yeah," he says on a sigh.

My eyebrows raise at him. "Why are you here?"

"Blake called and told me what was going on. Somehow, I convinced everyone at the station that this could be the end of Savage Temple, that this would be enough evidence to bring them down and take them out of their position of power. Everyone agreed, and we came as soon as we could."

"Thank you," Dolly tells him.

He glances around us, clearly looking for something else. "Where's Sadie?" His voice is so innocent, like she's probably hiding around the corner, afraid to come out in the open. My heart sinks knowing that he's going to be in more pain than I can imagine.

She turns in my arms, and I don't need to see her face to know that she's crying again. I can hear it in her voice when she whispers, "Rollo…"

"What?"

"We need to talk."

And then she spends the next hour explaining everything to Rollo, including how his girlfriend, their best friend, is dead. He did not take the news well, and all I could do was watch as he fell to his knees and wept into his hands.

CHAPTER TWENTY-NINE
DOLLY STERLING

RAIN DRIZZLES OVER THE CEMETERY, soaking the tombstones and drenching our raincoats. It's a typical Oregon mist that coats everything it touches. Fitting, because it matches my mood, my raw and dreary sadness. The rain mixes with the tears on my face to the point where I can't tell which is the elements and which is my grief. They mix together on my chilled cheeks.

Jagger and I stand hand-in-hand with Rollo on my side and Blake on Jagger's. All of us watch Sadie's casket get lowered into the ground. It's just us. The guys from the tattoo shop stopped by for the burial service but left shortly after the pastor to deal with their own emotions on losing a friend and coworker.

I couldn't part with her, I couldn't quite turn my back on her yet, and I don't think I'm alone in that. So we wordlessly agreed to stay and watch her casket for a little while longer, knowing that as soon as we leave, there will be eight feet of dirt forever separating us from her.

I know that's the wrong way to think of it. Sadie isn't in a body anymore. Sadie is wherever our spirits go once our body can no longer hold them. What's in that casket isn't my Sadie, and I know she wouldn't want me to suffer, thinking that if I leave the cemetery, she'll always be alone. But right now I just need a moment to wrap my head around it. We all do.

Rollo and I split the cost for this small funeral, covering all of her expenses, and yet, it doesn't seem like enough to repay a woman who saved me from being sexually assaulted. A woman who might as well have been my sister. But I suppose I saved her life in the past, and then she went ahead and saved mine. It doesn't soothe me that this went full circle and one of us ended up dying in the end anyway. That's just something I'll have to make peace with.

The casket is dark-stained oak with floral designs etched into the wood. She'd hate it. I know she would, but I don't give a shit. She deserves pretty things because she was a pretty soul. She didn't deserve the life she was given, a life a secrecy that hid away a horrible past filled with a lifetime of pain and suffering. She deserved the best things in life, and because her life was stolen so soon, the least I could do is give her the best at her funeral.

"It doesn't seem right," Rollo whispers from my side. He and I both have moved past the sobs and screams of the last few days to an uneven acceptance that she's gone. We have each other left, and surprisingly, Jagger isn't stepping in the way of that. He recognizes that we're close, and I have yet to see him feel threatened by it.

I grab Rollo's hand and give it a squeeze. "We'll get through this."

He pulls his gaze away from Sadie's box and gives me a sad smile. "We will." With a deep sigh, he releases my hand and looks past me to Jagger on the other side. "Have you guys talked yet about what you're doing with the Temple's property?"

I cringe, because we actually haven't yet.

Everyone in the Temple was arrested, and the children were handed over to the state. Neither Jagger nor I care about what happens to the adults. They deserve everything they get. But we were reassured that the children would be well taken care of until a judge can decide what to do with their parents. As of right now, all of them are being charged with child abuse, child endangerment, sexual abuse, and several more crimes that should land them in jail for a long, long time. I don't feel sorry for the adults, but I worry over the children. I don't want them to live a life like Sadie and Jagger had when they ran away all those years ago. I don't want them to be afraid and confused and always looking over their backs.

His father's body was found buried on the property, deep in the woods. Rollo is the head of that investigation per orders from his captain, but I have every faith that nothing will become of it. No one is at fault for his father's death but the father himself. However, since this made headlines, Rollo has to do everything by the book.

As for his sister, she was cremated. Jagger will get the ashes soon, and then we'll head to the mountains where he can spread them among the freedom the landscape provides. She'll officially be free. It's a beautiful thing he wants to do for her. Even if she was who she had become, she hadn't always been that way. She was all Jagger had at one point in his life, and he wants to celebrate that side of her. And me? I'll be there every step of the way with that for him, helping him navigate the grief of officially losing every family member in his life.

I don't know what happened to Sadie's father's body, and frankly, I don't give a shit. Rollo had a lot of questions about the condition he was found in, and I wasn't afraid to supply all the answers. Jagger filled in the rest—the part that everyone in the Temple liked to overlook about Tyron. In the end, I could tell Rollo agreed that he got everything he deserved. He wasn't allowed to say it, but I could see it all over his face how angry he was.

And the property itself? His father had left it in his children's names, and since Issy is gone, all of it belongs to Jagger, including the money that was in the Temple's savings. That's what Rollo is asking about, because at some point, Jagger has to make some hard choices.

Jagger drags his bottom teeth over his top lip. "The money will be evenly distributed into medical funds for the children of Savage Temple. I assume there is someone you can appoint me to for that? I want them all to have the money they need for the therapy they'll need."

Rollo nods. "I know a guy or two."

"As for the property, I have a few plans for it."

"Care to share?" Rollo asks.

"He won't even share with me," Blake grumbles from his other side. "You will tell me though, right?"

Jagger looks down at me and rubs his thumb along the back of my hand. "I have some discussions to have with Dolly first before I do anything, but once I have her approval, I'll let you know."

"Sure, man," he grumbles again. He slaps him on his wet shoulder and strides back toward the cars. "Whatever you say," I hear him add. He'll be fine, I'm sure of it. Blake has been around a lot the last few days, making sure everyone has the support they need. He's a good guy, and he takes great care of Jagger, but he's feeling a little lost now that Jagger doesn't need the attention that he used to.

"You don't need my permission to do anything," I tell him with a scowl. "This is your property, your memories, your pain. I'm not going to tell you how or what to do with it."

"This is our life." His voice is deep and rumbly, almost like thunder. It makes my insides warm. "Your opinion means everything to me, and it will have a voice here."

"Jagger," I begin, but he leans toward me and presses a soft but quick kiss on my lips, effectively shutting me up.

"Well, I hope you do something good with it," Rollo murmurs. He glances one more time at Sadie and then takes a reluctant step backward. His mouth moves, and I can hear murmuring coming from him, but I don't understand a word. Perhaps he's praying. Perhaps he's telling her goodbye. Whatever he's doing, I let him do it in private.

I let go of Jagger's hand, kiss my palm, and blow it toward Sadie's casket. I whisper, "I love you," before I turn away from her. It's painful, it feels like I'm leaving her behind, but I take one step after another. The further I get, the easier it gets.

Jagger follows me before twining his fingers once more in mine. I sniffle a little, and we're silent all the way to the truck.

Raindrops trickle down the sides of the truck. Like a gentleman, he opens the passenger door and allows me inside, then travels around to the driver's side and hops in. The engine roars to life, and semi-warm air blows in our faces, providing much-needed heat to our chilled skin.

I rub my fingers together to gather some warmth, and then I ask the question I've been dying to have an answer to since the first time we were alone. "Jagger?" He glances over at me, and he slides the truck into gear. "Do you regret killing your sister?"

He blinks at me once. Then again, before his brows pinch together. "That wasn't my sister, Dolly. I still regret leaving the sister I loved behind, but I do not regret killing that thing that was threatening my girl. No." He shakes his head in emphasis. "No, I don't regret killing her. Not for you."

"Why?" I whisper because I need to know.

He reaches to grip my chin, then he pulls my face toward his. There's a precious moment when he gazes into my eyes, and then he gently kisses me before whispering against my lips, "Because I love you, I choose you, and I want you."

My heart races in my chest, and a blush rises to my cheeks. Until now, Jagger's never been able to utter those words. I don't even think he knew how to form them, let alone knew that that's what he was feeling. But now? Now it's a real thing, out in the open, hanging between us.

"Got it?" he adds, and I nod.

Kissing me one more time, he pulls away and begins the drive out of the cemetery. I'm shocked at myself that I've never gotten bored with Jagger. Jagger will never be a normal guy, however, not like my exes that I helped heal. I may be good for Jagger, but he'll never be fully healed. He will always have his issues, and perhaps that's what keeps me interested and engaged, but deep down, I know it's because I've never connected with someone like him before. I've never had someone complete me, or even complement me. We are two halves to a coin, and without the other, we are nothing.

I expect Jagger to turn left toward my house, but instead, he turns right. "Where are you going?" I ask.

"I want us to both be on the same page about the property," he states, and there's a lot of weight to it, a lot of seriousness in his tone. "I want to show you what I'd like to do with it."

CHAPTER THIRTY
JAGGER VALENTINE

"YOU KNOW," Dolly begins next to me, her tone unsure. The rain has stopped, but her hair is soaked by now, and it sticks to her face. She gently tugs it away and tucks it behind her ears. "This isn't what I thought you were going to do."

In front of us, my father's house is ablaze with bright orange fire. It took quite a bit to get it lit while it was damp, but I ended up starting the fire inside. It's a big *fuck you* to the entire Temple, one last middle finger to my father. I hope to God he can see it from hell.

A ding sounds from my phone, and I pull it out of my pocket while Dolly picks up some random debris and chucks it at the flames. Sometimes I have to remind myself that I'm not the only one who wants to see this cursed place razed from the ground and completely destroyed. I think she's getting as much satisfaction out of the fire as I am.

I peer at my screen and see that it's a text from Blake.

BLAKE

You love her, don't you.

It wasn't a question. The past few days he's been making a lot of new statements as he settles into a role he's never had with me before. He's just a friend now. I no longer need that caregiver that he's been for me, and I think that makes him feel a bit lost. Dolly has told me to give it time, that it'll work itself out.

ME

More than anything.

BLAKE

Have you told her?

ME

Yes.

BLAKE

Lol. That doesn't sound like you.

ME

I'm not the same man anymore, Blake. You and I both know that with her, I'm better. I will spend the rest of my life showing her how grateful I am for her, and if I need to, I will tell her how I feel about her every waking second.

BLAKE

Dude, it's like I don't even know who you are anymore.

I smile down at my screen.

BLAKE

Fuck, this means I have to find a girl now that I'm not taking care of you.

ME

Probably.

BLAKE

Does Dolly have any friends?

I chuckle, shaking my head, and pocket my phone once more.

Dolly turns to face me with her hands on her hips. "So, I get the fire thing, but what do you plan to do with this place?"

I reach, grab hold of her from around the waist, and tug her to me. Her hands rest against my chest and she peers up at me lovingly. For the first time ever, I feel like I deserve that love. "I'm going to demolish every building, clean the slate, and then start an organization that helps stray or unwanted pets and those who suffer from mental illnesses."

"What?" She cocks her head to the side. "Like matching a dog with a person kind of thing?"

"Exactly." Pride fills my chest. It was an easy decision. "Cats, dogs, even ferrets if we so choose." Though I'd prefer no ferrets. They're just rodents that someone brought inside.

She raises both of her eyebrows. "I like that."

"Me too." I slip my hands under her jacket, then beneath her shirt, and skate my palms across her warm, curvy back. I then lean in close and whisper in a purring voice into her ear, "But that's not all I have planned for this property."

A shiver racks her body. "Oh?" she asks breathlessly as I dig my nails into her flesh, teasing with a little pain.

I bend my neck a little further and press my lips to her skin, kissing my way up to the hollow behind her ear. "Mmm," I hum. I run my teeth over her earlobe, and the way she moans has my cock stiffening. "Darling?"

"Yeah?"

"Run," I growl.

She doesn't hesitate. She bolts from my arms and races toward the woods far behind my father's house. I watch her go, feeling that desire—that predator's instinct—to chase down my prey. But before I do, I turn and look at what I inherited, breathing in the smoke from the fire as I do. I may have a shit ton of bad memories of this place, but I sure as shit can turn it into something good. It doesn't have to be a place of hate. It can be a place of healing. For me, for Dolly, for all the people we're about to help. This is what my real sister would want. This is what Sadie would want too. And truthfully, this is what I need.

A future, I realize. I'm going to have a real one. I want that for us. I was some semblance of normalcy. I may not be able to give Dolly the white picket fence and all the diamonds in the world, but I can give her me.

Am I enough? Absolutely.

I used to wonder if that would ever be true, if I would ever be enough for someone as I am. If I were worthy of it. Dolly has shown me that I am. She doesn't have to tell me, she displays it in every action. And here I am, with that same woman allowing me to hunt her down like some animal, and I know that she loves me with everything that she is. That's all I need from her, and that's all she needs from me. Being present. Being loyal. Being true to who we are as individuals and as a couple.

A grin widens over my face as she disappears into the first line of trees. I take off my jacket, drop it to the wet ground, and race after the woman who has my heart.

"You know this is forever, right, darling?" I holler after her.

A LOOK AT BED OF ROSES

BOUQUET OF LIES BOOK 1

I'm afraid of death.

Working at a funeral home will do that to you. And when my parents died, that fear became impossible to ignore. I needed out. A clean break. So I ran to a forgotten little town in Utah where no one knew my name.

The rental was cheap, a so-called *fixer-upper*. I didn't mind the work. But no one warned me how bad it really was—shattered windows, Pepto-pink toilets, peeling yellow wallpaper. Oh, and the bloodstains on the floor.

Or that the last tenant *vanished without a trace.*

They also didn't mention the man sent to do the repairs: brooding, intense, hot… and freshly released from prison.

AVAILABLE NOW

USA TODAY Bestselling DV Fischer is a mother of two very busy boys, a wife to a wonderful and patient (thank god) husband, an owner of three sock-loving German shorthairs, and slave to a cat they pulled out of a dumpster (literally), Geralt. Together, they live in Sheldon, Iowa.

When DV Fischer isn't chasing after her children, she spends her time typing like a madwoman while consuming vast amounts of caffeine. Just kidding. She can't do that anymore. One cup a day or she regrets all her life choices for the next twenty-four hours.

Known for the darker side of imagination, she enjoys freeing her creativity through plus-size romance that may only exist between the pages, no matter how much we wish otherwise.

www.dvfischer.com

www.ingramcontent.com/pod-product-compliance
Lightning Source LLC
LaVergne TN
LVHW040218110826
845146LV00005B/1336

* 9 7 9 8 8 9 5 6 7 6 4 7 9 *